Glass Elevators

By Mary Anne Martin

Glass Elevators   Copyright 2017 Mary Anne Martin

This book is intended for entertainment purposes only. Any resemblance to persons, living or dead is purely coincidental.

This book is dedicated to Ryan, Jayson, Jessica and Alex, the best there is. They make my life wonderful and keep me on my toes.

Glass Elevators

CHAPTER 1

If one more person smacked him on the shoulder and said everything was going to be okay, Mac was going to do some smacking back. *It* wasn't *okay*.

Lifting his eyes from the three fingers of scotch in front of him, he attempted to focus on the mirror behind the bar. The image reflected through half empty bottles wasn't pretty. He looked like blurry hell, which was exactly how he felt.

Behind him a swarm of regulars jockeyed for position. Same scene, different bar, or was this the same bar he'd been in last night? He wished to God the humming in his ears would drown out the tinny voice scratching his ear drums.

His eyes slid sideways, then down over black silk swatches barely covering unnaturally large assets. One of those assets was in danger of popping on his shoulder if the woman it was attached to pressed any closer. His gaze crawled up to her face pausing at puffy red lips stretched to expose blinding white teeth. Slashes of color pointed to dark eyes circled in black, shocks of platinum blond hair framed it all. Mac bit back a smile, the woman looked like a raccoon that got a hold of a cherry pie. He was sober enough to keep that particular thought to himself.

"Are you gonna drink that or just stare at it Sugar?" Raccoon's voice pierced the hum again and buzzed around in his head. Another face fell toward him just beyond her, or was that the same face times two? It was tough to tell.

Mac blinked to clear his double vision, then downed the liquid fire in one gulp. There were still two women looking at him when he refocused.

"This is my friend Stacy, she's a big fan too." Raccoon said.

"I'll bet." He mumbled, figuring he'd about had it for the night. "I'm gonna head up…" He didn't finish his sentence because both women attached themselves to him like clinging vines before his ass left the seat.

"Could we both get an autograph or somethin'?" Raccoon's friend asked, emphasizing a *somethin'* that had nothing to do with his autograph. And hell, who was he to argue with a request for *somethin'* like that?

Catching one girl under each arm as he spun on the stool, Mac waited a beat for the room to catch up with his eyes before standing. As he navigated the bar, a few fans called out that he'd played a great series, some questioned the umpire's vision and parentage, but others argued that Mac's luck had run out. He ignored it all.

"Don't listen ta those jerks Mac baby." The raccoon's voice ripped through the air again. He stared down at her plump lips and hoped to God she wasn't a talker, or a moaner, that nasally twang would kill him if he had to listen to it for too long. Fortunately, he could think of ways to keep that mouth busy…no talking involved.

He was halfway through the lobby before some of his fans were documenting his evening on their cell phones. He veered right and headed toward the closest available elevator. The clear tubes that rose up through the center of the building didn't provide much privacy, but neither did the fishbowl he lived in, the doors were open and waiting.

Stepping in, he turned to face the control panel and drew a blank, what the hell floor was he on? Ten? No not ten, maybe it was twenty something? Thanks to a convention, he'd moved from a suite with unobstructed views of the New York skyline to a room in a sister hotel, whatever the hell that meant. This sister hotel had a view of a few tree tops, the busy sidewalk, and the cement wall of the building across the street. To make matters worse, he was in a room barely big enough to fit a bed, TV, and small table and a chair. The mirrored doors of the elevator slid toward each other just as a woman skidded to a halt in front of them. Big green eyes locked on his for a split second before his reflection was staring back at him.

Mac's brain froze. He cursed, peering through the side of the glass enclosure as it began its ascent. A primly dressed woman with fingers pressed over her lips as if she'd just seen a ghost glanced up over her shoulder then hurried away. His heart sank to his feet.

Pushing away from Stacy and Tracy or who ever the hell they were, he hit the stop button, and when the damned car didn't stop, he hit it again a dozen times.

Glass Elevators

"Where the hell is down?" The elevator ground to a halt and the doors opened midway between floors, setting off an alarm.

Mac cursed again as he scanned the lobby below. She was gone. She'd probably never been there at all. He had too much to drink, and his mind was playing a game. The same old game it always played, but it was getting more absurd as time marched on. The woman in the lobby was blonde; she'd never dye her hair. Or would she? He blew out another breath. When the hell was it going to end?

Stacy and Tracy were staring at him as if he'd just told them that their favorite plastic surgeon was going out of business. He put a finger over the talker's lips before she could utter a word. Mac breathed deep and reached for a smile to reassure them that everything was just fine, then he hit another button and the elevator moved again. "Thought I forgot my favorite pen," he joked, but didn't feel much like laughing, "and you both wanted my autograph, or *somethin'*?" He drawled and wiggled his brows, earning him adoring stares once again.

Mac briefly considered the timing of his vision and dismissed any thought that started to form when Tracy? blinked up at him and asked about the size of his bat, or did she want him to sign a hat? Draping his long arms over the women's shoulders, he hoped the mini bar in his room packed more then a mini shot of scotch.

Seeing JJ again, even imagining her, was too damned sobering.

He fished his key card from his jacket pocket and slid it in the lock. The room was dark but for the dim glow of the streetlights not too far below. He liked the view from the penthouse much better. One stinking pitch and he was reduced to a room in a sister hotel. It was impressive enough for Stacy and Carla though, or was it Tracy and Tina? He really didn't care, both were looking up at him like he was a god.

Who wouldn't want this life?

Jillian Leigh struggled for breath. Keeping her steps short and rhythmic despite her aching feet, she pulled her coat tight and refastened the suede belt as if it was holding her together. The effect he had on her wasn't right. It just wasn't fair. But life isn't fair, she knew that better than most people.

Jill avoided his baseball games, refused to watch his interviews and turned off the news before they showed his highlight clips, even though 'Mac' McInnes was a walking highlight. According to all of the sports channels, and most of the major networks, everything he did was news worthy. The entertainment channels loved his antics, and frequently aired his adventures as if there wasn't anything else going on in the world.

Once in a while she forced herself to watch him play, and each time, she found her heart swelling uncontrollably. Then reality would strike and shred it to pieces again. More often than not, he was tied to some gorgeous woman who he was having a bawdy public fling with. Jillian would endure the sordid details as a reminder that they both made choices long ago, and there was no such thing as 'what if' in her life anymore.

Glass Elevators

What was the boob still doing in New York? Didn't he fly back with the rest of his team? Or was he above all of them now too?

Her reaction was ridiculous; she wasn't a naive kid anymore. There was nothing, absolutely nothing left of the man she knew who shared the same body as the sleazy millionaire baseball player in that elevator. She was worth just as much as he was, and she'd earned it on her own, without the help of him or anyone else, and she hadn't sold her soul to get it. A pang of guilt pounded through her heart, she may not have sold her soul, but she'd lost a big piece of it.

Rising to the top of her field hadn't been easy. She spent hours studying people until she knew every nuance, mood and movement that made up who they were, or more importantly, who they thought they were.

Pictures, her pictures, often captured what others missed, or wouldn't dare shoot. Her unremarkable features had preserved her anonymity while she was out capturing images that would become imprinted in the minds of millions who saw them and read her concise, no holds barred articles with the byline, PJ Storm. At first, her online audience enhanced her print following, but now people demanded instant access to information 24/7, it was exhausting keeping up with the life she made.

No other photojournalist accomplished what she had while preserving their anonymity. PJ Storm simply didn't exist in the real world. Some women used their assertiveness and beauty to get ahead, Jill used her ability to blend into the woodwork to climb the success ladder one difficult rung at a time.

Glass Elevators

She learned a long time ago not to put all her eggs in one basket, and while photo journalism provided for her well, opening a home improvement and craft store '*I Did It Myself*' blossomed into more than she ever could have imagined. In the four years and seven new stores since, hundreds of employees turned their lives and futures around with her help. She still preferred her camera to a boardroom, so her sneakers and work boots still got more wear than her pumps and heels.

'I Did It Myself' was expanding again, though Jill had reservations this time. The typical hectic hustle and bustle life of a New Yorker didn't usually leave much room for crafts, building dollhouses, painting, or sewing quilts. Though the market analysts she'd met with didn't agree. People wanted the comforts of affordable homemade things again. With the fluctuating economy,

and so many people in danger of losing their jobs, being self reliant and able to do minor home repair work yourself was an advantage people needed. The free classes geared toward small repairs, sewing and painting were usually booked solid, and judging by the demonstration clinic they'd given earlier in the day, maybe her initial thoughts had been off about opening a store in Manhattan.

    Jill stopped her frantic pace; her feet were swollen and throbbing. She made the mistake of scouting for possible subjects for her next project while wearing the same uncomfortable heels that plagued her feet through a full day of meetings and presentations. There'd been no time to change her shoes, her clothes or take the darn wig off that always felt like it was smothering her brain cells. Pantyhose that were supposed to massage her tired legs and provide her with energy to last eighteen hours, were pinching in some places and sagging in others.

She pressed her hand over her growling stomach and glanced at her reflection in a darkened window and couldn't recall if she'd consumed anything other than four cups of coffee all day. A couple holding hands passed behind her and shared a private laugh. She couldn't remember the last time she'd held someone's hand like that either.

JJ shook her head, who was she kidding? There was no time for sitting down to a decent meal, let alone time for a relationship. She'd been there, done that, and been thoroughly destroyed by it. It just wasn't in her cards. Who wanted to spend time with a woman who had no time to spend?

Glass Elevators

The two women in the elevator had time. And they were obviously what *he* wanted, probably what *he* always wanted. In fact, Mac McInnes wanted anyone that wasn't her. Both women he had his arms around were stunning, and obviously, star struck, and she was just a plain Jane who no one noticed unless they had to.

Jill moved closer to the window for a better look at herself. Staring back was a successful woman who followed her own advice, did what she loved, and loved what she did. Jillian Leigh wasn't helpless or dependent on another living soul, especially not Galen Michael McInnes the crowned prince of baseball. And once she washed what was left of her make up off her face, changed out of her stuffy business attire and let her hair breathe, she could be herself again.

Glass Elevators

She headed back to the hotel absorbing the sights and sounds of the city that never sleeps. Tantalizing aromas wafting out of dozens of restaurants had her stomach growling. The bright lights above and the interesting people she passed whet her appetite for adventure, stirring her imagination.

Her feet protested every aching step she took.

She should have gone up to her room and ordered in, even if it meant taking that elevator with *him* and his *choices*. By now she'd be wearing her slippers and sitting down to a nice dinner.

Just seeing *him* sent her into a panic, and she ran. Ok not ran, but left the premises, and was now paying for it with aching feet and a growling tummy. Being in the same room with *him*, or in an elevator with *him* and his little clingy friends might just push her normally sensible self to do something rash. She couldn't put her finger on just what that rash thing might be, but it probably would be embarrassing.

Jill laughed pitifully, and turned to catch sight of an old man sweeping his little section of sidewalk. He probably did the same thing every night for years. Her imagination kicked in as she wondered about the sights the man had seen through the years and the people he'd met. Maybe there was a story there.

A frown crept across her lips as her thoughts slid from one idea to the next. Without a doubt, she was headed for another bout of insomnia. Though her work output was phenomenal, and she had more ideas than she could ever implement, her sleepless nights were starting to worry her. The insomnia was becoming increasingly worse, and she needed quality sleep soon. The two-hour catnaps she'd been living on weren't recharging her batteries nearly enough, as evidenced by her complete over reaction to *Mr. Mac Superstar*.

Maybe one glass of wine and a quick bite to eat before going up to her suite would help her relax enough to get the sleep her body needed. She still couldn't bring herself to take those pills the doctor prescribed, and hated the thought of resorting to medication.

Jill stopped at the hotel's Sweet Nothings Lounge instead of the five-star restaurant on the opposite side of the lobby. It was an average bar, with the usual flirting and subtle touching going on. Pick up lines and semi sincere promises rumbled around the crowd gathered at the bar, while piano music came from a platform in the corner. A few clusters of people sat at the tables dotting the room.

She turned her head instinctively at the mention of *his* name, then scolded herself for trying to hear what the group of men were saying as she waited for her glass of wine. There was no danger of running into Galen again. Mr. Superstar seemed to be rather happily occupied for the evening. He probably never saw her earlier, no less thought about her.

If he wanted to get in touch with her, he would have never let seven years go by without so much as a word. She knew for a fact he had his chances to make contact.

Glass Elevators

CHAPTER 2

Mac opened one eye, when the light slicing through the part in the curtains didn't blind him, he opened the other and took a quick peek around the room. He was alone. The raccoon clones were gone, but left in their wake was one zebra striped thong draped over the head board and some sort of feathery thing that he couldn't quite place, or remember anything about. It must have been a very entertaining night. Bits and pieces of the evening were fuzzy. And if he really thought about it… he was probably better off not thinking too hard about anything yet, lest his head explode. Tracy and…whoever, were nice enough, they wanted exactly what he wanted; a bit of fun, no commitments, no attachments, no promises. They'd have a story to tell their friends and so would he, if he could remember it.

What he did recall was that the clones kept some extremely skilled cosmetic surgeon very busy, and whoever he was, (and he was certain it was a man who created the perfection), he was good. Not a single thing about either woman was real, not the ample breasts, perfect noses, wide lips, flat bellies, perfectly rounded backsides or hair color. It still baffled him that a woman would go through all of that pain and money to enhance themselves. But what the hell did he care? The results were spectacular. If the trend kept up, pretty soon women would all look alike. What would the clones look like in another thirty years? He bristled at the picture that crept into his mind of a puzzle with pieces that didn't quite match, yet fit together to make a whole. Would the new parts deteriorate? Need replacement? Did they come with a warranty? He pulled a pillow over his head when it all got to be too much and his brain throbbed.

JJ is real.

Damn it, there she was in his head again.

He didn't want real. Real let you down, caused pain, and left opened wounds, something he couldn't afford again. The last time was too much, and it nearly ruined him. Yet, no matter how many women he met, no matter how many women he dated, or slept with, he always thought about *her*.

Then came the emptiness.

Glass Elevators

Unfamiliar scents that were intriguing in the haze of the night, always became repulsive by morning. Big green eyes and the face of an angel haunted Mac's thoughts as he showered. He toweled off, tugged on a pair of threadbare sweat pants and a shirt with the sleeves torn off, then stepped into his old running shoes, pulling the laces tight.

A run would rid him of those haunting green eyes and fill the emptiness in his gut. He reached for three aspirin, swallowed them with a gulp of water, pulled on a cap and sunglasses and left for the streets of Manhattan.

For someone who had it all; money, cars, fame and freedom, he looked pretty pathetic. But every morning he ran from it all until he could finally draw a breath without a prickle of loss in his heart, then, he ran right back to it like an addict in need of a fix. Maybe one day he'd just keep running.

When he ran, he wasn't Michael McInnes, or Mikey, or Mac or whoever they wanted him to be. He was just a regular guy out for a run. It reminded him of where he came from when fame made it easy to forget.

The season was over, and unlike the previous three seasons that had produced sizable bonuses, unending accolades and more endorsements than he could imagine, it ended with a loss.

And losing was unacceptable.

The loss was his fault, making it an even tougher pill to swallow.

He watched strike three whiz by with the bases loaded and him feeling like hell.

Glass Elevators

The pitch was a strike and he was out, regardless of what people thought they saw. He knew it before the umpire made the disputed call. Still Jim Talbot, his manager, argued until his face was beet red, believing with all of his sixty-one-year-old heart that the umpire blew it, and that Mac should have been awarded first base on a walk.

Mac remained silent on the matter through post game interviews and questioning looks from teammates. The pitch was nearly perfect, right where he liked it, and he froze.

There was no game winning homerun, no single to score the runner on third, not even a freakin' walk. He watched the final pitch of the series hit the catcher's mitt behind him. The guy didn't have to move his glove an inch.

Glass Elevators

The young pitcher looked like a deer in the headlights when Mac stepped up to the plate, then nearly flipped cartwheels after the strike three call. Even Drew Madigan, the all-star catcher took a moment to comprehend what happened before he ran out to congratulate his rookie pitcher.

The loss ate at him, but he stayed in the place of his defeat to take the edge off before going back to start the cycle again in preparation for next year.

Stacy/Tracy and Carla/Carol scratched an itch, but they didn't fill the gaps, and his life had become full of gaps. Mac pulled up short. Maybe it was time he considered a change of pace, maybe he should…what? Find a nice girl to start a relationship with? He huffed out a disgusted laugh, then turned the corner and headed across town wondering if maybe today was the day he'd keep right on running.

Enjoying the brisk pace of the city and the enticing aromas drifting off of the food carts dotting the sidewalks, mingled with the distinct smell of mid autumn, Jill paused to shoot a picture of a woman who looked remarkably like the dog at the opposite end of a gem encrusted leash. The blonde cocker-poo was peering at the latest issue of Fancy Dog magazine, while the woman scanned the cover of Beautiful You on the newsstand shelf.

After spending the early morning documenting the less appealing side of Manhattan, Jill set out to find the counterbalance, the good, or the whimsical. Just as she had in her other photo essays, she chose to show the city's whole personality, not a skewed version.

She backed away to get another shot, and bumped into hard mass.

"I'm so sorry," she called without glancing back. Her subjects in focus and framed well, Jill continued to shoot.

"Sorry." Whooshed out of the jogger's mouth as his hands briefly steadied the preoccupied woman's shoulders. His fingers tingled.

JJ.

Mac stopped as if he'd run into a wall. Determined to put a stop to the game his mind plagued him with, he spat out an oath. Peeling his dark glasses off he turned to face the woman who couldn't possibly be *her*, though everything inside him told him she was.

Glass Elevators

    A chestnut ponytail was half tucked into her hooded sweatshirt, as the woman abruptly straightened and went stiff as a statue, the rest of the long-gathered tresses spilled out. He forced his legs to take a step toward her just as a group of tourists converged on him. Three young boys held out slips of paper while older fans thrust maps of Manhattan at him to autograph.

    Jill knew without a doubt whose body she elbowed, heat spread through her system like a wildfire. She turned slowly, pointed the camera on impulse, and snapped frame after frame of a stranger she once knew better than she knew herself.

    He looked much like the boy she'd fallen in love with so long ago. Spikes of dark hair fell beneath his old college baseball cap, his sweats probably hadn't been washed in weeks, and the sneakers he wore had more holes than material. The man in her viewfinder was smiling, though his eyes told her he wasn't. Jill's breath caught when those familiar wolf-like eyes turned up and found her, as if the camera and the crowd were non-existent. The image of the boy faded while his eyes bore into her soul with an unflinching stare.

She looked just like he remembered her, with a camera blocking most of her pretty face, intense eyes searching to find the right mood of a shot.

A pen was thrust into his hand, so he signed his name blindly as she snapped another picture, and hid behind her camera. He inched toward her, and she retreated well beyond the crowd surrounding him.

A woman pressed forward and stole a kiss from the star, Jill's camera clicked, and unexpected nausea rose in her throat. Disgusted with her reaction, she lowered the camera and turned away. She cursed herself because she should have gone to sleep last night after the single glass of wine, her head would be much clearer now. Instead she stayed up watching the Food Channel, and wound up hunting down a 24-hour diner at 4am. The Pass the Buck Diner's Specialty; bacon, eggs, cheddar cheese and hash browns wrapped up in a buttermilk pancake looked just too good to ignore on TV while her stomach grumbled over the few pretzels and peanuts she choked down waiting for her glass of wine.

"JJ!" Mac called to her over the din, "Don't go."

Jill hesitated, then turned to face him, shaking her head. The irony of his words cut. Those had been his final words to her once before, although then they were preceded by an ultimatum.

His eyes pleaded as he spun his hat brim backward, and a hopeful smile lit his face. She closed her eyes and pressed her lips together, willing the courage to do the right thing, because the wrong thing would hurt, and hadn't he hurt her enough?

She studied the cracks in the sidewalk. There were no answers popping up, just discarded gum and a glittering gem from the cocker-poo's leash. Jill dragged her eyes back up to meet his, Mac's brow rose in question as his head tilted to the side in an unspoken plea. She watched him for another minute, then blew out a breath. She was being a sentimental fool, but maybe after all this time they could be civil.

She shook her head in mock disgust.

"Galen! What do you think you're doing? Are you impersonating that baseball player Mike McInnes again? You know how much trouble that caused last time." Jill took a step toward the crowd and shook her head at him like a mother scolding a child.

"Galen?" Someone called out with a foreign accent. As one, the crowd looked at Jill, then the man she was shaking her head at.

Mac's arms dropped to his sides. He did all he could to keep from laughing wildly. JJ still had her crazy imagination, intuition, and she was even more beautiful now than he remembered. That playful little smile she was trying to hide was stirring emotions he forgot he had.

"Galen." Mac shrugged and nodded. The pen he'd been scribbling autographs with was snatched from his hand. "Sorry, people make that mistake all the time."

Glass Elevators

His fans looked down at his indiscernible signature, tossed slips of paper to the ground and folded their maps muttering curses. Some studied his face again before dispersing.

For a moment, Galen was the man she saw, and it surprised her. Jill fought the desire to go to him, and then the conflicting urge to run away. She took a deep breath, and swallowed hard. When the masses parted, he stood facing her as the rest of the city moved around them in a blur.

"You remembered." Mac smiled like a shy schoolboy and tugged his brim forward again. "It's good to see you JJ." He wanted to pick her up and kiss her senseless. But a wall was already going up between them again, one that had fallen for a moment.

"How could I forget? It's good to see you too." She managed to get the words past her lips without sounding too cautious. There was so much she wanted to say, so much she wanted to ask him. But most of all, she wanted to run.

"You look…beautiful, JJ." He closed the gap between them and brushed a kiss on her cheek, the familiarity came rushing back like a wave. Her scent wrapped him in a warm embrace before his arms slid around her in a hug that felt too right. He looked down as her face turned up to his, and for a moment everything stood still.

She smiled, "How many fastballs have you taken to the head Galen? I look about as beautiful as you do right now." She tugged at her sweatshirt, and messy ponytail.

"This look happens to be one of my favorites." He said.

Her smile faltered. "I know."

He lifted the camera that was caught between them. "You still…?"

Jill nodded.

A crease formed between his brows, then disappeared as he lowered the camera to dangle around her neck.

"I'm sorry about your loss the other night." Jill was reaching for something to say. Anything other than the hundred questions that played over and over again in her head like a broken record. Or the excuse to leave that was dangling on the tip of her tongue.

"Did you see the game?" He sounded like a little kid hoping for a piece of candy from the dentist.

"I was in a meeting." She hated the thought that she was disappointing him. "But I saw the end of it."

His eyes lit up, and he laughed. It figured she'd catch his not so finest moment, and, if she saw it, she knew the umpire was right. "It's ok you can say it, it was a…"

"Strike, and right where you like it." A warm familiar pattern began to weave around them again. Her nerves were settling and the excuse to leave fading.

"Yea, the perfect pitch and I let it go." He looked away, then found her doing the same. "So, what are you doing in New York? Is this home for you?" He asked to fill the distance his last statement created. He didn't want distance now, not when he'd just found her. He wanted answers to questions he couldn't bring himself to ask. Questions he gave up the right to ask.

"No." She answered quickly. "I'm here on business, I've been in meetings all week, I was just out playing with my camera before the next one." Her eyes wouldn't meet his until she finished speaking. "I think we may be staying at the same hotel."

"The same hotel." He repeated. Shame bowed his head before he could meet her eyes again. "So, it was you last night, in the lobby."

He was drowning. Pulled under by his heart and soul, and he couldn't pool enough resources to fight it. Feelings he'd forgotten existed rushed over him until his heart was pounding so hard the old man in the newsstand on the corner could hear it. She was slipping by again, just like that pitch.

Jill nodded numbly, a picture of him with the two women in the elevator sprung into her head. It froze there, and the warmth that spread through her system turned to shards of ice and sliced at her.

Emotions she'd long ago buried clashed. She shut her eyes and demanded control. When her lids lifted, he was staring down at her, sucking in all of her air and allowing her to suffocate while he took his fill and more.

A large shaky hand reached out and touched her cheek, catching the stupid tear that slid under her radar. This isn't the way she wanted him to see her, not even close.

Galen's eyes fell to the drop of moisture on the tip of his finger. His thumb closed over it, testing its validity.

"JJ you're crying." The woman of steel was crying? Galen reached for her as confusion overwhelmed him, "What the…hey, I'm sorry. I…"

"No, don't. It's my allergies acting up, I'm late…I have to go." Jill stepped back like he'd just slapped her, then turned and walked away.

Mac's stomach pitched as if he'd just been dealt a blow by a prizefighter. The city suddenly felt too small. He needed to go somewhere he could think, because for a few moments, standing on a busy street corner in the heart of New York City he felt as though he were alive again, and it was going to kill him.

Glass Elevators

CHAPTER 3

Galen Michael McInnes stared out the window. Somewhere down in that jumble of people, JJ was hurting, and even though it seemed impossible, his gut told him that he was responsible for her pain.

Glass Elevators

It made no sense, they hadn't seen each other in years, and he hadn't yelled or demanded answers or accused her of almost destroying him the way he figured he might if he got the chance. In fact, they were very civil, *too damned civil* if he really thought about it. But he didn't want to think about it, he couldn't, his brain only focused now on that damned tear.

He didn't think JJ knew how to cry. But there on the street corner, after rescuing him from 'his public', she cried. He looked down at his fingers, the ones that brushed her tear away. It was gone, but it had been there, he saw it, he felt it. And now all he felt was empty again. He wasn't buying her allergy excuse; she had no allergies that he knew of. The exception being the one she developed to him seven years earlier.

The bottle of scotch sitting on the table was tempting, but he needed a clear head. Mac braced his arms on the windowsill and rested his forehead on the smooth glass. Savoring the cool feel of it, he closed his eyes and rolled his aching head from side to side.

Seven years.

Seven years he lived without her.

He made something of himself. Hell, he'd made a whole lot of something, and he didn't need her. His hands balled into fists on their own in disagreement.

Mac slowly opened his eyes and low and behold; there she was again, walking toward the building as if she was debating each step. She stopped at the corner, and looked up before crossing the street. For just a moment he thought she might have seen him, but that was ridiculous.

Glass Elevators

    He glanced over at the newly made-up bed, he hadn't slept much last night and now the aspirin was wearing off. What he needed was sleep, then he could think more clearly. Seeing JJ had simply sent his body into an old conditioned response, no better than a typical teenager. He could have a whole harem of women, he didn't need her. She walked away from him *again*, and made him feel like crap to boot. It was obvious that she wanted nothing to do with him, he was as sure of that now as he was his own name. Or, maybe not, the ache in his heart held a sliver of hope that she would give him a few more minutes of her time again. He swore at himself with his next breath. "Yea Gale, you've really got it all together don't you? Shit."

    An old irritation resurfaced. What kind of parents named their kid Galen? Did they want him fighting his way through school daily? Galen certainly didn't suit a professional baseball player either, but Mike did, and Mac was even better.

He changed his name as soon as he was called up to the majors, and except for JJ and a few close friends, no one had called him Galen again. But he liked the way she said *Galen*, like it had honor, as if the title 'Sir' preceded it.

She'd said it that way out on the street, and drove the crowds away with it. Then she cried, and what the hell was that about? He didn't think she had tear ducts. She fell out of a tree once and broke her arm in three places and didn't even whimper.

She didn't shed a single tear when she walked away all those years ago either.

Mac sat on the bed, then turned and punched at the feather pillow before falling back on it. He laced his fingers over his head and pressed down squeezing a flood of memories away.

His eyes closed for a minute. Just a few minutes of sleep would help the pounding in his temples. His thoughts drifted until he fell into the dugout of his high school field, he'd just rounded the bases hitting home plate in stride and was being slapped on the back and high fived. He quickly looked toward the fence where JJ was clapping frantically, a clunky 35mm school camera draped around her slender neck.

"I got it Galen." JJ mouthed to him. "The instant you made contact." She pointed to the camera. A rush of first love's sweetness filled him, overriding the pride of hitting another homerun.

Making sure none of the other guys saw him; he pointed and mouthed, "That was for you." It was JJ's birthday.

Her smile made him blush. One look from her could melt his heart in an instant, causing a swell of desire not conducive to playing baseball.

He watched as she ran and retrieved the ball from the woods behind the outfield fence. After the game, she had him autograph it, so that, according to her, when he was rich and famous she could sell it for a few thousand dollars. Bobby Harris added his signature to the ball, because according to him, if anyone else were playing first, most of Gale's throws from shortstop would be errors instead of the amazing plays they were. Besides, Bobby insisted, he was going to be the one to make it big, so it wouldn't be worth a dime without his signature on it.

A shrill voice called out in his dream, "JJ you get that skinny ass home now. I made dinner." JJ's backyard abutted the school fields, and her stepmother had a habit of screaming out the back door and embarrassing the hell out of her.

Mac tossed and turned, fighting the uncomfortable invasion of Sylvia LeBuntoski's voice. At least he'd had his grandparents to care for him, and though they struggled to get by, they loved him, and did the best they could by him.

His dream flashed to his grandparent's smiling faces as they were pulling out of the driveway in their old Chevy to go to bingo, an image that was burned into his memory forever. The two people that loved him, and he adored, waved goodbye and drove down the road. It was the last time he'd seen them alive.

Three days after his eighteenth birthday, and two weeks before starting college and fall baseball, Galen Michael McInnes became a homeowner, with all of the bills and responsibilities that entailed. The weight of the world was heavy when you were just eighteen and alone.

Despite his coach's insistence that he move into a dorm, he remained in the small house he inherited. It was just five minutes from campus. Bobby Harris moved in with him and helped with the bills.

Bobby came from a good home. His parents loved him but didn't have a clue that the seventies had been gone for quite some time. Bobby made most of the major decisions about his life since he could put sentences together. His parents were good-hearted hippies that never grew up. They supported Robert's call to freedom and provided their son with a nice little Jeep Grand Cherokee to get around in after he convinced them that he was looking into converting that particular model into a ecologically friendly recycled fuel burning vehicle. Bobby had no intention of changing a thing about the car, but made sure he hit a fast food place before stopping at his parent's house so the story smelled authentic.

JJ moved in a month after Bobby did, avoiding a move to Georgia with Sylvia the alcoholic, and the latest deadbeat she hooked up with. Sylvia didn't bother to conceal her feelings when JJ decided to remain with him and Bobby. She always considered the girl to be a burden and made Cinderella's stepmother look like mother of the year.

If Sylvia's parting words were meant to cut JJ, they didn't hit their mark. But he silently damned Sylvia to hell for telling JJ what an ungrateful bitch she was.

JJ smiled and wished Sylvia happiness as the taxi pulled away from the curb. She was either a great actress, or made of steel. She told him it took all kinds of people to make the world go around, and if you never saw the bad, how would you recognize good? There was nothing good about Sylvia so far as he could tell, except that she moved out of town and left JJ with him.

It only took JJ minutes to unpack the few things Sylvia hadn't claimed. It killed him to watch her fold the crumpled clothes she hastily tossed into two brown grocery bags as she put them away. A small purple bear he'd won at a carnival, a seashell they'd found at the beach, and a wood box that he'd made in shop class with her initials carved into the top of it were placed on top of her dresser. It was all she had.

JJ was thrilled to finish high school in the same place she started. The school administration vaguely knew about her situation, but never did anything about it. JJ was a good student and a sweetheart in all of her teacher's eyes. There were plenty of kids that caused trouble and wrecked havoc with the school's desire to rank in the top echelon, there was no need to disrupt a good student's progress by looking too deeply into her background.

Bobby signed anything JJ needed a parent or guardian's signature for, and no one ever checked to see exactly what that signature said. The three of them took care of each other just fine.

Mac's dream jumped to his first year of minor league ball, JJ's face danced in front of his dreaming eyes again lit with happiness, "Your coach called…Oh, Galen, I think it's good news, I just have the feeling…" She was hugging him so fiercely he ached.

Then there she was sitting in the stands watching batting practice at his first major league game. She'd cut class and drove three hours to be there.

Next, they were at a party she put together when he signed with California and received a substantial pay raise, boosting his annual income into the millions.

"We don't have to struggle anymore." He said and spun the small opal 'friendship ring' on her finger, then took it off, replacing it with a three-carat diamond, and laughed when her eyes almost fell out of her head. "Let's get married now."

"Oh Galen, I can't..."

"You can't? You already said you would." His stomach sank.

"No, not... I can't that, I can't this." She tugged the ring off, and reached for her opal. "It's too big, what if I lose it?" Her hands shook as she replaced the opal on her finger. "I love this one, you gave me this one when you proposed the first time."

"But you deserve this one JJ, we're moving up in the world. Hell, we're on an express elevator heading for the penthouse; I don't want people to think I can't take care of you." He watched her silently debate. "You can wear this one on this finger," he moved the opal to her right hand, "and this one on your left hand." He held both hands up for her to see. "So, what do you think?"

"It-it's beautiful, thank you." She was shaking, her voice a whisper.

He held her close and kissed the top of her head stilling her trembling hands in his. Her reaction scared him.

"What's the matter Baby?"

"I-I don't need this ring." She looked so deeply into his eyes he felt as though she touched his soul. "I just want you. I love you Galen." And he knew she spoke the truth, the warmth of it surrounded him. The desire to possess her, protect and cherish her filled him once again.

Images fast-forwarded through laughs and precious moments never to be duplicated, her smile tripped his pulse again when she'd tugged him out to the old porch swing and told him she had some good news.

She received a grant because of her excellent work in photography. He lifted her right off of her feet as pride swelled in his heart.

Then the world slowed as she clung to him and spoke those fucking words again "...I have to travel to Africa and the Middle East for ten months, but it's the same months you'll be playing and traveling too. I won't be here alone without you, so you don't have to worry about me getting to and from my classes and all. Oh, Galen I can't believe it! Isn't it exciting?"

Her words spilled out in rapid fire, but his brain stalled catching only bits and pieces.

...She couldn't believe someone liked her work other than him and Bobby, and they were biased anyway so their opinions didn't count...She was so lucky she was picked...a privilege...maybe she could make him as proud of her as she was of him…the chance of a lifetime…

She was beaming when he settled her to her feet. JJ of few words and deeply controlled emotions was ecstatic, almost the way she was when he'd first asked her to marry him. Energy flowed through her and shot out in all directions. He felt the buzz from her joy, but he'd shut down already.

He felt sick as his dreams began to lift enough for him to remember what he was going to say. The words never changed, no matter how much he wished they did.

Again, his mind's eye watched her face melt as the words spilled out of his twenty-four-year-old mouth. "Tell them no, you're not going. It's too dangerous."

Glass Elevators

His dreams darkened. He walked in a fog of anger and spite, where images were unfocused, until his parting words a few weeks later.

"If you go, I won't be here when you get back. It's either me and all I can give you, or that damned camera. You don't know what you're getting yourself into JJ, this isn't taking pictures of some damned squirrel in a tree, and look at what happened then, you broke your arm doing that. We're talking guns and bullets over there JJ. You think you'll be safe, but there is no such thing over there. You're safe here, where I can take care of you. You don't need this. If you get on that plane we're done. Don't come back."

He saw himself toss his packed bag over his shoulder.

"Come to New York to watch me play tomorrow, after that I'll be on the road for two weeks." He saw the hurt look on her face but said the words anyway. "I'm telling you JJ, don't go."

He closed the kitchen door behind him, but not before he heard something clink on the counter. His dreams faded to black. There was always nothing after he uttered those words, yet night after night he said them.

He woke with a start, disgusted with himself, then rolled over and buried his face into the pillow again.

After the unsettling day Jill had, she was looking forward to dinner with Bobby Harris. Four years earlier they'd run into each other when she called the law firm

Glass Elevators

Harris, Stone and Feeney to assist her with a business matter.

The shock of seeing each other at their first meeting had made it difficult to concentrate on anything but a reunion. Both threw caution to the wind in front of assistants and partners and simply held onto each other for a good five minutes before mentioning business. After the brief morning meeting, the two took the rest of the day off and caught up on each other's lives.

Since then, no trip to the city was ever finished until they met for dinner, or lunch.

Now that Bobby knew all about her other career; he called if he knew she'd be leaving the country, just to read her his riot act. Old habits were hard to break.

After looking through the clothes she'd brought and dismissing most of it as too businesslike, or overly casual, JJ held up a little black dress that her assistant Stasha insisted was a necessity. It was plain and simple. Casually neat, just the look she needed for the restaurant downstairs.

The silky material was a tad clingy, but it was soft and felt good. Jillian ran her fingers over the pearls she'd bought when her first pictures were published. They were elegant but not too flashy, just what she was looking for.

Bobby Harris wouldn't show up at a garage sale looking anything but perfect.

Jill glanced over at the foot killing heels lying next to her suitcase and groaned in anticipation of putting her rounded toes into pointed shoes again, then grinned mischievously and reached for her black flats. They were really slippers that looked like shoes, and unless someone grabbed her feet and examined them closely no one would know.

With all of the major meetings finished, Stasha wasn't here to nag her, and Bobby wouldn't recognize them as slippers. After a five-minute search yielding only one of the comfortable flats, Jill conceded, and slipped on strappy black impossibly high heels that Stasha had put into the garment bag with the dress. Stuck to the spiked heel of the shoe was a scribbled note; 'Just in case'…whatever that meant.

Lately Stasha was getting a bit quirky. She was probably getting tired of being the face of *I Did It Myself* stores. JJ couldn't blame her. Poor Stash was like the Gerber Baby of the self help chain, and was almost always recognized. Jill couldn't risk her image splashed all over the place even with the wig and daily make over.

Instead she played the roll of Stash's assistant and right hand representative during most meetings and negotiations. Not that Stash was a slouch in the world of business. The woman was a dynamo.

Jill pushed back the curls of hair that fell forward during the fruitless search for her shoe and brushed off the lint that clung from the rug. At least she hadn't torn her stockings again. After another quick glimpse in the mirror, she grabbed her black leather clutch and headed out the door.

Through the glass elevator she watched people coming and going in all directions, it was like being suspended in the air. Everyone looked to be in a rush to get to someplace important, like bees in a hive.

The elevator stopped and the doors opened, and for a nanosecond *he* popped into her head again. Jill stepped aside to let an older couple join her for the rest of the ride down. Behind them, a tall dark and handsome type stepped in, his deep brown eyes slid to her legs then moved up slowly. The elevator moved with a start. Jill cursed the heels under her breath as she wobbled.

"Whoa, you ok?" One strong hand held her hip the other grasped her elbow.

"Yes, thank you." Jill raised her eyes to meet his. "Bobby."

"Jesus, JJ it's you." He looked down at her, studying her face.

"And had you looked at my face when entering the elevator, you'd have known that right off the bat." She teased him.

"You look…gorgeous."

"And so do you." Jill reached to straighten his nearly perfect tie and finger press his lapels without thinking. "Meeting a client on another floor? Or were you just so bored today you thought you'd joy ride in the elevator?"

Bobby looked up and rolled his eyes. He wasn't about to mention who he'd just spoken to, not yet anyway.

"Actually, I ran into an old friend, and may have just made a nice little connection." The elevator stopped and emptied, they were alone.

"So, I'll assume she was too busy for dinner tonight. Or will you be eating light?"

"You think you still know it all. She is a he, and I was referring to a professional connection, a new client. Not all of us can get shot at and take amazing pictures to make the big bucks." He slid his eyes to her looking for a reaction.

"I'm still in one piece Robert. And thank God you don't take pictures for a living, no one I know is interested in paying a dime for various angles of your thumbs, or unidentifiable blurs."

"Yea well, that was a long time ago, I've gotten better." He paused a minute. He must have hit a nerve if she was calling him Robert, so he went with it. "You said there was a close call in Libya."

"I didn't say there was a close call." She studied him for a moment, narrowing her eyes. "Have you been wooing Stasha into talking again?"

The moment of hesitation answered her question.

"She didn't tell me anything I couldn't drag out of you sooner or later, and I don't do wooing." He said.

"It was nothing."

"JJ your definition of nothing and mine isn't even vaguely close. *Nothing* in my book doesn't include being shot at."

"I wasn't hit." She said.

"This time." He drew in a deep breath. How could the woman put that cheesy smile on her face and say that as if she was talking about playing dodge ball?

The elevator came to a halt, and the two of them stepped out together.

"You think we'll have snow for Christmas?" JJ was done talking about that aspect of her life.

The aspect that just might get her killed one day, and he was damned if he'd stand by and watch her do it.

"Yea I think we'll have a regular blizzard." Sarcasm and a hint of annoyance tangled in his voice.

Bobby held the door of the restaurant opened for her. Plan A had failed miserably. Getting Galen to move to the same hotel JJ was staying in seemed like a good idea, then Gale went and picked up two groupies before they finally ran into each other. What a mess. He had higher hopes for plan B.

He returned her cheesy grin, and used his best bad French accent to guide her through the door. "After you ma-dam-wa-zell."

Bobby addressed the maitre'd who had a broad smile for Jill. The short stocky man motioned for them to follow him to be seated.

"Thank you, Walter." Jill tossed a smile over her shoulder as she sat.

"I'll give you one thing JJ, you can pick a good restaurant. They're not the same cooks who provide the room service here." Bobby smiled at a waitress passing by, then winked. "Last week…" He trailed off realizing the small confession he'd be making.

"The eggs were runny and the bacon rare?" Jill laughed. "And why would you be staying here Bobby?"

"Because it's convenient."

"You live five minutes away." She persisted with a smile on her face.

"So, do you think it's going to be a cold winter?" He opened the menu and closed that discussion.

The waitress standing near bit back a smile before approaching their table, she'd waited on the couple before, and they were usually quite amusing. The consensus in the kitchen was that they were a brother and sister, but some thought that they were an amicably divorced couple who still cared about each other enough to share dinner or lunch when in town.

"I'll have a..."

"Cup of coffee with half and half and two sugars, and a glass of white zinfandel. I'll have scotch neat." Bobby dismissed the waitress without taking his eyes off of JJ.

Through his mind floated pictures of emaciated children, and men standing in the background pointing guns. The pictures were so clear and detailed it looked as if the AK47 was going to be fired at the reader as he turned the page of the magazine. Bobby shook the image away.

"I saw the article you did over the summer. It was great, how many death threats you get since it came out?" He asked.

"None."

"I heard the threats JJ, that Kwaswani Mitusi asshole wasn't happy you exposed his little 'steal the food from the mouths of babes and sell it for weapons campaign' he won his last *free election* with." Bobby looked up from his menu. "There's a price on PJ Storm's head again...or should I say still?"

"Are you finished?" Jill stared at him. It was so damned easy to fall back into a long-forgotten routine, but they weren't in high school or college anymore. She didn't need him to protect her from the world.

"I'm sorry JJ, I have no right, I don't know what got into me." He placed the menu down and splayed his hands over the leather cover in a display of frustration. He knew exactly what JJ's driving force was, and whether or not she wanted to admit it, it was time someone did something about it before she took one too many chances with her life.

Bobby watched as her wheels spun. Jill smiled overly wide to hide her concern about the matter. "How did you know I didn't want tea and Merlot? People change you know." She said.

"Not much JJ, although I'm rethinking *that* now." He studied her hands over his, they were so small, yet so capable. He turned his hands over to squeeze hers and blew out a breath. "You really want tea and Merlot?"

"No, coffee and zinfandel." She laughed, "Most things are perfect the way they are." Jill pulled her hands back as the waiter arrived with their drinks.

She took her coffee cup first, filling it to the brim with half-and-half from a small silver pitcher, then added the sugars, stirring it with a musical clanking rhythm. After tapping the spoon on the rim twice and placing it face down on the plate, she drank the entire cup in two long gulps. She pushed the cup aside to reach for her wineglass.

"You cut back on sugar I see." He observed.

"Of course."

He blew out a long breath and settled in his seat.

"Did I tell you that you look beautiful when you dress like a grown up?"

"Yea, I do that now and then, you know at work, meetings, and when I send my jeans to the cleaners." Jill said, and sipped her wine glancing around the room at the couples who only had eyes for each other.

"I wasn't talking about your stuffy prim business suits I usually see you in. Or when you pull your hair back so tight it looks painful. Is that wig really necessary? And those glasses? Could you have picked out uglier frames? I mean I get what you're doing, but geez…" Bobby shook his head. "You look like you're a million miles away JJ." Bobby tilted his head trying to get a better read on her then followed her eyes to a couple. The guy was slipping a ring he probably couldn't afford on the smiling girl's finger. When he looked at JJ again she was searching the menu.

"Mm-hmm." A flash of sadness passed through her eyes, before she focused. "I'm sorry Bobby what were you saying?"

"You just agreed to chuck it all and come with me to Barbados for the rest of the year as my love slave."

Jill reached over and took his drink from him. "I have to remind the wait staff not to put hallucinatory drugs in your drink until after you've paid the bill."

"I did say dinner was on me didn't I?"

"After the kept man act you pulled last time, dinner is always on you." She folded the menu and reached for her half empty glass. "So, what's up Bobby? You said you wanted to talk to me about something, other than my hobby."

Plan B.

"I sold the house." His eyes reread the menu for the third time, then glanced up at her.

She froze with the wineglass halfway to her lips, then pretended not to care and took a long sip.

"The old house, on Storm Street." He finished just in case she had any doubt about what he was talking about.

She considered what he'd just told her then frowned. "Galen sold his grandparent's house?"

She brought up Galen's name, something that had been taboo between them. JJ knew Bobby and Galen had remained close, and she didn't want to interfere. It became a don't ask/don't tell policy between them.

Galen on the other hand, had no idea that Bobby ever had any contact with JJ. At JJ's request he'd kept their reunions a secret from his best friend. He was stuck in the middle again, reminding him that the more things change, the more they stayed the same.

"Yea, to me a while ago. I don't use it, and I got a great offer for it. The buyer wants to close in ten days." Now he did look at her.

If he didn't know her so well he'd have missed just how much that information hurt her. She'd become even better at covering up her emotions than she was when she was younger. He once swore the girl had no tear ducts, and emotional control Special Forces could use as an example.

"They really like the place?" She finished drinking the contents of her glass. "Do they have children?"

"No. I think the guy just wants it to use as a rental property, you know off campus housing. He'll probably divide it up and rent out the rooms to some poor college kids who will be grateful to be out of the dorms." He repressed a smile. "I think I'm going with the prime rib."

Jill bit the inside of her cheek to keep her mouth from opening up and yelling at the unfeeling oaf across the table from her. "And you're telling me this because?"

"You asked." He said with a grin.

Jill closed her eyes in frustration, willing patience. He was toying with her somehow. She knew that 'I can't look JJ in the eye' thing Bobby did whenever he had something up his sleeve. Or when he was avoiding something, like a little boy not wanting to tell his mother he just rode his skateboard into her garden.

"Oh." She'd play his game for a few minutes.

Their waitress took their order, smiling at the couple like she had a secret. When Jill ordered another glass of wine, Bobby figured that she was taking the bait.

"If there's anything you want up there, at the house," he swallowed the last of his scotch, "it's yours. You left some of your things there back when. I think one of your old cameras is still there, and there are some boxes in the attic with your name on them."

"Galen didn't get rid…my things are still there?" She asked, sounding surprised.

"As far as I know. I rented it out for a while, but as of last week, it was all still there."

The waitress refilled Jill's glass then left the bottle.

"I should have brought it down for you, but I was a little pressed for time." He eased back just a wink.

"Ok, I thought that maybe you'd like to go up there before it's not available. Jeanine asked for you, she thinks you're avoiding her."

"I would never avoid your sister, and she knows that, I explained …"

"No, no nothing like that, she just misses you, I think that guy she was seeing, Jake dumped her."

"That jerk dumped her? I told her that he wasn't good enough for her. Did she tell you what…?" Jill stopped abruptly.

There were some things a girl did not want her older brother to know. It had been hard enough for Jeanine to tell her that Mr. Wonderful borrowed her car to get home in the morning to his live-in girlfriend, then swore that he broke up with the girl for good, only to pull the same stunt a few days later.

"What?"

"I'll talk to her, I'll make sure I call her tomorrow morning."

"JJ is there something I should know about?" He asked.

"Yes." She blinked. "That I would never rat out Jeanine to her bully of a brother. She's twenty-one."

"That doesn't help." Now Bobby motioned for the waitress to bring him a refill. "I know what I was like at twenty-one."

"She's not you. Girls are different."

"Not the ones I knew."

Jill rolled her eyes and laughed. "Oh, the ones you knew were very different. Jeanine isn't like them. I promise, she is nothing like most of the girls you brought home."

Home.

The little house Bobby was selling was the only place she ever truly felt was home. Even her new house with its five bedrooms, stone fireplace, gourmet kitchen, and sixty-four acres nestled in the hills of Pennsylvania wasn't home. It was simply her house.

"Maybe I'll go up to see her. It's been a while since we talked face to face. Not since the last time she was visiting you." JJ Said.

Bobby pulled a thick brass key from his pocket, and placed it in the center of the table. "You can stay there if you'd like. It'll be like killing two birds with one stone. Then you can tell me if I have to go Jake hunting."

She wrapped her fingers around the dull brass key and caressed the worn metal.

"If there's anything Jake has done that I have to tell you about, I'll be in need of your professional services to bail me out of jail first." She said.

Bobby smiled. She was going back. He hoped she'd forgive him later, but that was a risk he had to take. It was time to move on, and change the subject.

"Remember that little red head girl who followed me around until I finally asked her out, then she said no?"

"Meredith Haskins wasn't that little, she graduated only two years after me."

"Yea, well apparently, she still has a thing for older men. I ran into her last week. She's a very wealthy widow, three times over. Her dearly departed husbands' ages total two hundred and sixty-four."

"Wow."

"The guy she was draped around looked to be about one hundred and ten." Bobby watched JJ laugh, and hoped to God he was doing the right thing.

As dinner progressed their chairs moved closer, and reminiscing mixed with stories of the lives they lead now. They talked through dessert and coffee and then a few more drinks. Neither noticed that they were the last ones left in the restaurant save the staff. They agreed to split the bill after an amusing discussion ending with a hefty tip for their exhausted waitress.

In front of the door to Jill's room, they stood in awkward silence for a moment, neither wanting to let go of the trip down memory lane they shared through dinner.

"I had a nice time, one of the most relaxing evenings I've had in a long time. Thank you, Bobby."

Glass Elevators

Jill didn't know whether it was the wine swimming in her head, or familiarity that felt so good, like being home again, but she didn't want the night to end yet.

Bobby smiled and dragged a finger down her soft cheek, she was still beautiful, inside and out, though she'd never believe she was.

Her life had not been an easy one, but she never complained or sat back and brooded. At the ripe old age of seventeen she was on her own with two immature wise guys to raise, and help get through college.

It was JJ who took care of him and Galen, bailed them out of trouble, and made sure they both survived to receive diplomas. She'd make anyone who cared to listen believe it was the other way around. And he loved her for it.

Bobby was sure that he knew only a small portion of what she endured in her early personal life, the other stuff she hid or used as motivation to push the limits.

The three of them survived with only each other for so long that they'd become a family, sticking together through thick and thin, until the realization of their dreams came to be. Instead of cementing their relationships, it tore them apart. Even his success hadn't brought the comfort that his friendship with JJ and Galen had.

"Be safe JJ." He kissed her forehead and stepped back before he did something stupid that would run the risk of ruining what they'd rebuilt. Though it would be easy, too easy in the state they were both in.

"I will. I'll return this to you before the end of next week." She ducked her head and held onto the key she'd once left next to her engagement ring when she left the house on Storm Street that last time. "Thank you, Bobby, for a really nice night." She finally looked back up at him. "And for being a really good friend."

The Sweet Nothings Lounge was a crowded for a Saturday afternoon. Bobby walked in dressed to kill. He took the stool next to Mac and ordered himself a club soda and Mac whatever he was drinking, which lately had been too much scotch.

"Hey. Sorry I'm late, I had to take care of a few things." Bobby apologized then did a quick scan of the room looking for a diversion.

"Things?" Mac asked.

"Business. Hey, I sold the old house, and I'm closing in a week. Before I have it all hauled off, there's a few boxes you left behind. You want the stuff?" He popped a few pretzels into his mouth.

"You sold it?" Mac asked frowning into his glass.

"I never use it, renting it out is a pain in the ass." Bobby's eyes roamed over the brunette next to him who seemed to be intrigued by a maraschino cherry.

"How was your dinner with JJ? Anything important come up in your little chat?" Mac took a deep gulp of his third scotch. "You two looked cozy in the corner, staying until they closed the place." He put his glass down and growled. "How the hell long have you known where she was?"

"You followed me?" Bobby asked.

"I couldn't figure out why you'd just stop in, no call, nothing. I knew she was staying here, I ran into her on the street. I put two and two together, and came up with one hell of a coincidence." Mac lifted a glass of scotch to his lips. "Well?"

"Well, my firm is involved with her company. I almost choked when I saw her wearing that little black number, I guess she gave up the jeans and sneakers look." Bobby smiled. "She's a successful business woman."

"Yea, I'm sure, a regular entrepreneur. A lot of good that damned grant did her huh?" Mac mumbled almost too quiet for Bobby's ears. "She still playing with her camera though, she had it with her yesterday." He sipped his drink. "I lost a girl to a camera, how's that for a laugh?"

"We're not having this conversation again." Bobby shook his head. "You didn't seem too worried back when. In fact, you were hell bent on banging every woman you met not more than a month after JJ's plane took off, and you haven't stopped since. Don't start having regrets now pal, it's a little late."

"I don't have regrets, look what she missed. I could have given her anything she wanted." Mac stared into the mirror behind the bar again. "It wasn't good enough."

Bobby laughed sarcastically. "You still don't get it. Did she ever tell you that?" He looked his friend in the face. "'Cause I thought maybe she felt it was the other way around. She wanted the one thing you wouldn't give her. But that's all in the past. She's moved on." Bobby looked at his watch as two women approached them tossing their blond manes over bare shoulders.

"She's married?" Mac asked.

"No." Bobby turned away to check out the woman behind him, barely repressing a smile as the brunet began nibbling another cherry. He turned back to the bar and threw a key on the glossy surface. "That's the key to the house, if you want anything that you left there, you have to pick it up this week. The sooner the better, the buyer is pushing to move in."

"You're really selling it?"

"You did." Bobby said with a bit too much vehemence.

Mac deserved that, after all, he'd sold the house after he realized JJ wasn't coming back and he couldn't find her when he finally tried to.

He covered the brass key with his hand; maybe going home again one last time would ease the nightmares. It was worth a shot to rid himself of JJ once and for all.

She wasn't looking for any kind of reunion, which proved his instincts had really gone to shit, he should have realized that when she didn't contact him for seven years.

How much of a jackass could he be? She checked out of the hotel first thing this morning, and went back to her comfortable life that didn't include him.

Or maybe she left to avoid seeing him again?

"I'm guessing that you're going to be staying on the East Coast for a while, saves me the flying time. Going to head to Greenport?" Bobby asked.

Mac hadn't thought much about his beach house out on Long Island, but it wasn't such a bad idea.

"Maybe you should spend a little time away from all of this Gale." Bobby referred to his friend the way he did in private. "I'm concerned about the drinking. I said I wouldn't say anything, but...I said it." He shrugged knowing where pressing the issue would land him. "I'm gonna run, busy day." Bobby smiled at a woman who just arrived and was hanging over his shoulder. "If you're going to go collect your stuff though, better go this week, otherwise some college kid will be using your old gloves as oven mitts."

Mac watched Bobby's reflection walk away with a Barbie clone attached to his arm. "Yea, busy day, Bobby."

Mac turned the key over in his hand, its warmth surprised him.

"To old times," he raised his glass and downed the contents. The image of JJ's face with a tear slipping down her cheek still burned in his mind. "And moving on." He amended.

His decision was made. She'd be out of his system by the week's end even if he had to burn all of that shit that he knew was still in that damned old house. Pictures, dried flowers from proms, empty wine bottles they'd shared, countless 'things' JJ had kept or given to him and he knew Bobby hadn't tossed.

Bobby was a sentimental sucker. Or, that's what he had been up until now. It was about time that Bobby gave up the asinine idea that they all should somehow "get together and talk". JJ most likely told him to go to hell if it came up during their four-hour conversation last night.

A muscle in Mac's jaw jumped as his teeth ground together. He left quite a few things back in that house, including one small jeweler's box containing an unwanted three carat diamond ring. Maybe that was the key, he knew it was still there waiting, when it was gone, she'd be gone from his dreams the way she'd been gone from his life.

He laughed at his reflection in the mirror. That jerk looking back at him sent flowers to JJ's empty room this morning.

With one eye on the brunette with the affinity for cherries, he formulated a plan. He'd head out to the beach house tomorrow and settle in for a day or so. He'd pick up his car, then maybe Tuesday or Wednesday he'd

Glass Elevators

take the ferry across the Long Island Sound to New London and drive home.

It wasn't going to be home much longer.

CHAPTER 4

Jill pulled up in front of twenty-seven Storm Street, parking her SUV at the curb instead of pulling up the paved driveway that ran into the back yard where a single car garage stood.

The house looked much as she remembered it, but better.

Bobby had it painted recently, probably in order to sell it. The clapboards had a fresh coat of maroon paint and the trim was a creamy white. Even the gingerbread trim looked new. The window boxes contained fall flowers stretching their necks for the ever-shortening daylight. Lace curtains hung in the front windows, and if she wasn't mistaken they were the very same curtains she made to replace the yellowed ones Galen's grandmother hung years before.

Jill glanced up to the second floor where her old bedroom window looked out over the small front lawn.

After she graduated high school, Galen had shared her bed most nights, or she his. But she kept her own room, and he had his. He told her once that he wanted her to know she'd always have her own space to come home to. Bobby occupied the master bedroom at the end of the hall, and he was frequently sharing his room with his girl of the week.

Heat rose in her cheeks. She'd lost her innocence and her heart inside this house. Part of her soul was roaming the rooms too. Facing her past would be therapeutic. She shouldn't still be blushing because of things that happened years ago.

When she checked in with Stasha, whose voice miraculously recovered from the laryngitis that had her running back to Harrisburg two days earlier, Stash suggested she take the whole week to visit her hometown. In fact, she all but applauded Jill's decision to take a short non-working vacation. The well-meaning butt-in-ski was more than capable of running things.

Jill opened her car door, then shut it quickly when doubt and fear hit. She was being ridiculous, sentimental and childish. The house was just a house.

The things she'd left there she'd lived without for years, she could just as well keep right on living without them.

But, in a week or so, it would no longer be available for a damned trip down memory lane, and, she promised she'd visit with Jeanine.

Jill got out and marched to the front door, key in hand. She left her two bags in the car, unsure whether she'd spend a few days to purge herself of Galen McInnes forever, or she'd just grab her things take Jeanine to dinner and find out what was going on, then head for the hills of Pennsylvania. She could make it to her house by one in the morning, maybe. Home, she could make it home, this wasn't home anymore, her house…HOME was in another state.

Bobby Harris sat behind his desk looking like the cat that just swallowed the canary.

"Thanks, Stasha, my sister will make sure she stays a few days. I think it's for the best, one way or the other. I was hoping they'd get together on their own, it didn't work out that way, so maybe this will." He laughed. "Don't worry, I'll take the blame. You're going to owe me dinner after all is said and done, and it's not going to be a McDonald's drive thru dinner, lady."

"We'll see who owes who dinner, if this blows up in our faces, I might not be able to afford Mickey D's." Stash said.

Bobby flipped a pen in his hand as he listened to Stasha's concerns about the backup plan they hatched. His eyes drifted over to the picture he kept of them sitting on the porch of the old house. "If this doesn't work, the two of them will continue to kill themselves trying to prove they're worthy of each other. I think you're right about that." He waited a beat before adding, "And Stasha, thanks for getting in touch with me. JJ has no idea." Bobby sat up as his partner came into the office and plopped down on the leather chair in front of his desk. "I'm gonna run, keep in touch." He hung up, but a crooked smile tugged at his lips.

"So, is it business or pleasure that has you here on a Saturday afternoon?" Rick Feeney toyed with the magnetic game on the edge of Bobby's desk.

"Neither." Bobby raised his brow.

"How'd it go with Mac and the craft guru."

"Moving to Plan B."

"I think you're nuts. Although, I never saw him freeze at the plate like that. That was a perfect strike."

Rick shook his head and tapped the desk. "If she's the reason, then more power to you, but, how the hell do you let a woman do something like that to your head anyway?"

"It's not just her, and she is not just your average woman." Bobby pulled the picture off of the shelf behind him.

"Yea right. Different name, different smile, hair color whatever, they're all the same in the end." Rick huffed out.

"Not this one. This one is a bit different. Beyond her guru status and hiding behind her assistant's face, she's got another real talent, with a camera." Bobby would trust Rick with his life, he knew he'd understand the importance of keeping JJ's secret "That little lady is PJ Storm."

Rick took another look at the picture he had in this hand.

"And that secret can never ever leave this room." Bobby said. "I'm not joking Feen, no one knows, and I need it to stay that way. She's like a sister to me."

Rick Feeney's stoic face slid into a picture of disbelief.

"You're kidding me. PJ Storm! This little girl is the one who took those pictures in Iraq and Serbia. Those pictures from Afghanistan?" He looked up at Bobby, the four people in the framed picture were young and full of life, Bobby's sister was the youngest and looking at the other woman with adoration in her eyes. It was obvious that they all cared deeply for one another. It looked like a family portrait. "I always thought she was a he. She got a death wish?"

Bobby took the picture back. "They both do as far as I can tell."

Rick grimaced. "I can see why his mind could wander, I don't think I'd want the woman I love out getting shot at." At the word love, Bobby's head snapped up. "How long did you say this has been going on?"

"It isn't going on, and that's the problem. And you just renewed my hope pal. If you think it's love, then maybe the two of them can figure that out too."

Stasha Robbins paced the cream-colored carpet of her office. She was doing the right thing wasn't she? Jill trusted her, and now she may have just set up her friend, who also happened to be her boss, for a heart wrenching experience.

Glass Elevators

It couldn't be worse than what Jill lived daily. She continually put herself in harm's way. Stasha was one of the few people who knew all about the multifaceted life Jillian Leigh lead. As her personal assistant, or as Jill called her, her life manager, she was privy to quite a few unnerving and gut wrenching facts about Jill. It was one of the reasons she agreed to be the face of the company while Jill did most of the work behind the scene. Not that Stasha didn't pull her share of the weight; she couldn't thank her friend enough for the opportunity she'd given her. But the more she learned about Jill, the more she knew that the woman's life needed adjusting. They'd become friends during what seemed the worst times in both of their lives, and bonded over misery and despair, but helped each other climb out of the pit and into the sunlight. Somehow Jill had left a part of herself in that ugly old pit of sorrow, and it was going to keep pulling her back until it swallowed her again if she didn't do something soon.

The lack of any real relationships in Jill's life was her first indication that Jill hadn't quite dealt with her past. Although there were a few poor choices that crashed and burned before making it to the runway, the only consistent company Jill kept was with herself. But the Jillian Leigh Story Book was left open and few lost chapters spilled out at her last Fourth of July party.

After all of the guests left the festivities, and the catering staff departed, Stasha stayed to help Jill clean up the few remnants, and talk. The two of them got tipsy. Well, she was tipsy; Jill was toasted, which was the equivalent to hell freezing over.

Glass Elevators

Once Jill started baring her soul, Stasha started drinking coffee, and replaced the wine in her own glass with ginger ale.

Jill, of few words and fewer emotions, was a real mess, more so than even she imagined.

Pieces of a puzzle started to form a picture of two young misguided souls who made decisions that they'd spent a long time regretting, but both were too stubborn to admit. Jill still loved the dumb ass baseball player who had given her some kind of ultimatum that he regretted, and had only made to keep her safe. Carrying around a torch for seven long years was a heavy burden.

After contacting Bobby Harris and discussing the matter, it seemed that the two misguided lovers were out to prove that they'd both been right, and would kill themselves to impress the other.

Glass Elevators

    Mac was doing a slow spiral into self-destruction with alcohol and pushing his abilities to the limit. Once in a while he'd have a quick flirt with death; driving his car like he was competing in the Indy five hundred, which lead to totaling three cars in a two-year period, two public brawls in the past six months, and a total disregard for his body when he played baseball.

    Both of the pig heads had changed their names, they claimed it was to help their success, but, if she remembered anything from her college psychology classes they were both also hiding behind their new identities.

    She abruptly stopped pacing. If only she had the confidence Bobby Harris had. Her perfectly arched brows drew together, if the plan didn't work, at least she'd get a nice dinner out of it.

She wished she'd taken the other side of the bet, because this plan had to work. Jill still had that sexy little black dress with her that Stash insisted she take with her. Too bad she'd wound up wearing it for the wrong guy.

Glass Elevators

CHAPTER 5

The key fit into the lock with a little twist and a jiggle. Jill pushed the door open and stepped into the house cautiously. The dark oak floors shone as if they'd been polished yesterday and there wasn't a bit of dust in sight.

Bobby must have had it cleaned, and was probably selling it as is, furniture and all. Didn't Galen want any of his grandparent's things? Or had he become too big for that too?

She slowly made her way in, picking up familiar objects, and skimming her fingers over one of her framed paintings that still hung in the same place on the wall. The house pulled her in, wrapped around her like a comfortable old blanket and warmed her.

She was home.

The wide kitchen window ledge still held colorful little bottles. Three empty wine bottles twinkled green, brown and purple in the fading sunlight, splashing color onto the linoleum floor. The place was spotless.

Jill was beginning to feel a little prickle of suspicion across the back of her neck. This was a house that was lived in by someone who cared for it. Just as she reached for the handle of the refrigerator to check her theory, there was a knock at the door.

Maybe it was the new owners to-be. She'd have to find her things and leave, and that would be just fine.

No, it wouldn't be just fine, she needed a little more time here, *at home*.

"Hello?" A female voice called from the porch through the opened door.

"Hello. I'm in the kitchen." Jill walked toward the voice.

"JJ?" A beautiful strawberry blond was throwing herself into Jill's arms before she made it to the door.

"Jeanine?" Jill wrapped her arms around Bobby's baby sister.

"I'm so glad you came, Bobby said you might. I cleaned the house just in case, I can't believe the blockhead is selling it. And there's no way I'd let your things go with the house, I told him…" Jeanine clamped her mouth shut. "Anyway, you're here!"

Jill held Jeanine at arm's length to look at her. "Yea, I'm here."

"You look beautiful, I love the updo, and is that a pair of heels?" Jeanine's eyes nearly bugged out.

"I came from an unscheduled meeting in Manhattan. I can hardly wait to get out of this outfit."

"Your room is still upstairs if you want to use it."

"Didn't Bobby rent the place out? It seems that nothing is changed." Jill had her arm around Jeanine as they walked to the front parlor, and sat on the old settee still draped with a blanket she crocheted. Jill fingered the holes and tried to ignore the dropped stitches she knew were hidden in the pattern.

"My darling brother rented the place to me. I just moved out last week. He thought it was a good idea for me to live here rather than campus housing, or God forbid, a sorority house while I was taking classes."

Jill laughed. How many times did Bobby bring one of the Omega girls home? Probably as many times as he hadn't come home because he'd stayed at the sorority house. His baby sister definitely wouldn't have her brother's blessing to live there.

"Was the rent reasonable?"

"The family discount; I cleaned it and did the upkeep, he was happy with the knowledge that I was safe and sound and only had a few parties now and then." Jeanine reached over and flicked on a lamp, the daylight was quickly fading to dark.

"So you're finished with school?"

"No, but I moved back with my parents…I uh, have a huge load this semester, and this, well, it's just less work to think about." Jeanine's stomach growled loudly.

"Hey you want to get a pizza or something? I haven't had a thing to eat all day. I can't stomach my mother's tofu and sprouts in its various forms three meals a day."

Jill beamed, and pressed her hand to her stomach, she hadn't been able to eat much of anything at lunch. Now however, she found herself starved.

"Sure, I left my bags in the car. I'd like to get out of this straight jacket and skirt first."

"So, you're staying a while?"

One look at Jeanine's face and her decision was made. "Is that ok?"

"It's great! My parents will want to see you too."

It seemed to Jill that Jeanine had a few things on her mind, and that was just fine. It had been much too long since she'd just gone with the flow. It had also been much too long since they'd spent time together.

All that lost time. Time that you can't get back.

Maybe they'd have a girl's night, with movies and popcorn and pizza. Something they'd done all those years ago, when Jeanine was just starting to notice that boys didn't have cooties, and Jill was head over heels in love.

If Jill was going on a trip down memory lane, she might as well walk down the whole road.

"I'll get your things, you can go up to see your room." Jeanine decided that sounded a little too pushy. She scrunched up her nose. "JJ, if you'd rather not stay up there, or you know, you can stay in my room down here. I took the room off the kitchen, it used to be the pool table room when you lived here."

Jill blushed at the thoughts that room dredged up. "Oh, no, no, that's ok. I'm fine with my old room, it'll be nice to see."

Jill made her way up the steps as Jeanine headed out to get her bags. She peered into the bathroom, it was neater than she'd kept it, and there were some new brass fixtures.

The next door was her room, she gripped the glass faceted knob and turned. The door stuck, and without thinking, she leaned her hip into it and he door sprung open. Floral potpourri filled the air. The room hadn't changed at all. If she didn't know any better she'd think it had been sealed off waiting for her to return.

Or that she'd just entered the Twilight Zone.

She moved to her dresser, and picked up the pictures one by one. Pictures she'd taken and long since forgotten about; Galen looking at her through eyes that said more than words ever could, Bobby holding Jeanine on his shoulders, and one picture that Bobby's mother had taken of the four of them sitting on the porch all looking very young and optimistic.

A bottle of Love's Baby Soft perfume sat on a crochet doily next to a seashell filled with fresh potpourri. Her small faded purple bear leaned sideways against the mirror. Two of her paintings hung on the wall between the two closets. She stepped on the lose floorboard, and just as she thought, it let out a yawning squeak.

Jill sat on the bed and slid her hand over the quilt she'd made using scraps of old clothes, and found Galen's number thirteen stitched on the corner. She'd taken it off of one of his old uniforms and sewed it into the quilt.

She stood up and the bed seemed to protest. The closet…was the secret door connecting her room to Galen's still there? She pulled open the right side closet door and froze, dumbfounded.

Jeanine stood in the doorway watching Jill's face pale, she dropped the bags, and rushed to her side.

"Oh. Bobby told me to leave it all. I knew I should have moved it out." Jeanine blew out a breath. "You didn't know about any of this, did you?"

Jill numbly shook her head.

"We didn't know where to put it all, there's more in the attic." She watched Jill. "He made a studio for you. The pool table went out the door to make room for it, and a dark room. It's everything you'd need for that I guess."

The closet was packed with boxes of lamps, and screens, film, trays, an enlarger, easels, and what she guessed was a state of the art computer for that time. There were tripods, and cameras wall to ceiling, a new sewing machine, brushes, spools of thread, wooden hoops, everything and more she would have needed for everything she loved doing.

"The other closet is pretty much filled with more of the same."

"Oh, Galen what were you thinking?" Jill's words were no more than a whisper.

"Are you ok JJ?"

Of course, she was ok. She had to be, didn't she? "Yea, I'm fine. Does Bobby want me to take all of this too?"

"I guess so, it is technically yours, if you want it."

She had no reply, she couldn't think. Galen made an art studio for her, and she never had a clue.

"It's starting to rain outside. Maybe I'll have Casa Leo's deliver a pie. You still like extra cheese and pepperoni? Maybe I'll get a few zeppoles too, and garlic knots. I have a few DVDs and a gallon of ice cream in the freezer." Jeanine said hopefully, not realizing she just gave away the fact that she still lived in the house.

"Neeny, I'm fine. It was just a surprise. You don't have to cheer me up. I know a prelude to 'If you're happy and you know it' when I see it coming." Jill hugged Jeanine close.

Jeanine was concerned about her, yet there seemed to be a conflict going on in her head, and she was tiptoeing around an awful lot. She'd just tipped her hand with the freezer confession. Why was Bobby selling a house that his sister was obviously very comfortable in? And if she guessed right, hadn't really moved out of.

"I wasn't going to break into that, I haven't done that song in…oh a week or so." Both women laughed.

"I'm going to get changed into something I can actually sit in comfortably." Jill sat on the bed and kicked her shoes off, then rolled her stockings down while Jeanine's face contorted into something from a horror flick at seeing the expensive shoes sail across the room.

Jill let out a sigh. "I can breathe." She reached in one of her bags and dug out a pair of jeans, then slid out of her skirt and tugged on the faded denim.

"You are going to hang that skirt and jacket up, aren't you?" Jeanine nearly drooled at the sight of the expensive designer suit in a heap on the floor.

Jill figured Jeanine was about the same size as she was, Jeanine might have to take it in a pinch or two, but as far as she was concerned, the suit should belong to someone who would appreciate it. "There appears to be no room in my closet, so…"

"Oh, no way."

"What are big sisters for?" Jill pulled a bulky sweater over her head.

Jeanine was staring at JJ now. She'd all but gulped back a horrified scream.

"JJ what happened to you? Is that a scar?"

Jill winced, she forgot about the mark down her back that ran parallel to her spine. "An old injury, it's nothing."

Nothing? Was the woman insane? Her skin looked as though it had been torn an inch wide and at least a foot long.

Jeanine let it go. From what Bobby had told her, JJ needed her family, and through default she qualified as JJ's family.

Jeanine needed her too. How many times had she wished JJ would just pop back into her life? And not just through the internet or phone lines. JJ was back for a little while, she wasn't about to lose her again so soon. "JJ, I've missed you."

Jill turned and hugged Jeanine again. "I'm so sorry Neeny. I should have come when you called about that jerk Jake."

"I'm over him. Can you believe I was so stupid? I kind of feel used. He lied to me and I believed him, even when I knew nothing he said was making much sense."

"You weren't stupid, sometimes your heart and your brain just can't get together and see what's really there." Jill said.

"Well, I found out what was really there the hard way. I thought he was so sweet. Shows what a good judge of character I am." Jeanine said on a sigh.

"Everyone makes mistakes, and except for choosing Jake, and your brother Bobby, although you really had no choice there, I'd say you're a good judge of character."

"You see, that makes me feel better, when I talked to Bobby about it, and I didn't even tell him half of it, he pooh-poohed me." Jeanine said.

Jill thought about what Bobby might do if he knew what had actually happened, and it wouldn't be good. Maybe that was why he was selling the house…if he really was selling the house. Maybe he was trying to protect his sister?

Who understands what goes on in a male's brain?

"Why don't you order that pizza, and I'll unpack a bit. Then maybe later you could help me sort through some of my things."

"You're gonna stay the night?"

"I'm thinking a girl's night in is a great idea." Jill said.

"Me too!" Jeanine nearly yelped. The hell with Bobby's plan, she was spending the night here. JJ needed her, and she needed a rational female to talk to. She'd go hide out at her parent's house tomorrow night. JJ might want company while going through some of the things she'd left here. Hell, if she were in JJ's shoes she'd want some support through a difficult time, even if it all happened seven years ago.

Men didn't get it. They never understood anything!

Mac stalked out of the lounge alone. It was barely five-o'clock, but he'd had enough. He shocked the shit out of the bartender by ordering a pot of coffee after Bobby left. He wasn't hanging around for another typical night in the life of Superstar Mac McInnes.

It was time to make a few decisions.

He needed to leave this all behind for a while before it really took control. He needed to think things through. Now.

Mac took the elevator up and watched the hustle of people below him. The two women he'd spent Thursday night with were sashaying toward the lounge with their blond heads pressed together. A big guy in a dark suit caught their attention.

Nothing, not even a passing glance from either one of them. Then again that's exactly what he wanted, wasn't it?

He packed up what he'd brought with him, and rode the elevator back down to the lobby. The doors opened to Carla and Tracy, or was it Carol and Stacy? They were draped around the guy in the dark suit who met him eye to eye.

"Hey, Mac McInnes right?" The guy he recognized as the Star's new quarterback grinned and extended his hand.

"Yea, you're Colin Mallon?"

"Yea. Sorry about that loss, you were robbed." Mallon said.

"Big game Monday night huh?" Mac shifted a bag over his shoulder.

"Yea." The quarterback draped his arm around one of the matching blondes.

"Good luck." Mac said and smiled at the girls.

"Thanks."

The two women smiled congenially and wiggled their talons at him, but turned their adoring gazes back to their new prey.

Mac settled his bill, and hailed a cab. The driver was less than happy when he gave him an address out on Long Island, but more than happy to make the trip when

Glass Elevators

Mac flung a couple of hundreds his way and called it a tip.

Traffic sucked, it always did on Long Island. The expressway was moving, but a lame pony tied to a plow could have moved faster. The swarm of pumpkin pickers that flooded the east end and forgot how to drive didn't help matters.

The beach house was dark by the time the cab pulled into the driveway, but as he approached the door the motion lights sprang to life. He found the key he kept in a lobster pot on the side of the house, too tired to dig through his bags for his own set of keys.

The woman he paid to clean once a week had done her job well, the place was immaculate, but it was cold. She probably turned the heat down. A fire would warm the place up and help him relax, because the cab ride was anything but relaxing. The driver had definite anger issues, and road rage took on a whole new meaning during the seventy-mile trek east. Mac swore the guy actually tried to run down a dear that was crossing the road in front of them. It was a good thing the animal could jump.

He checked the fridge, it was empty except for a few cans of soda, some bottled water and a twelve pack of beer that was probably a few months old. A peek into the pantry yielded better results. There were cans of vegetables, soups, some peanut butter, unopened saltines, a jar of jelly, canned stew, tuna and some Spam. There was some mix that required only water to make a mouth watering stack of delicious pancakes with, and an unopened bottle of syrup. Dinner!

After turning the kitchen into a war zone while cooking the quick and easy pancakes, Mac settled on the big overstuffed couch in front of the fire and finished his dinner. He located the remote control for the wall size television and began surfing. He paused briefly when a dollop of syrup almost hit the remote.

The weather girl was rambling about a storm making its way up the coast. He flipped the channel and found the end of a college football game that was played earlier in the day. Mac slid his plate on the floor and sank into the couch resting his head on the arm. He'd pick up some food in the morning. His eyes closed, and dreams took him back to Connecticut and JJ, again.

Jill laughed between bites of pizza as her favorite country singer crooned in the background. Jeanine was on a roll discussing Bobby's past girlfriends.

"…and when I met that one, I thought my brother had lost his mind completely. She was a loon too. I'm beginning to think that crazy IS his type." Jeanine rolled her bright blue eyes. "What is it with men?"

"If I knew…" Jill didn't have a chance, it seemed that Jeanine had quite a bit to say.

"The guy I dated before Jake, Kevin, thought that a date consisted of me picking him up, and me paying for our burgers at the drive through, and then hunting for his friends all night." She took a breath finally. "But Brent is different. He makes me laugh." Jill looked up at the change in Jeanine's tone. "We've only been seeing each other for a week, but I really like him. I've known him for a while, but just in a friend sort of capacity, lately though I think it might be something more."

Jillian knew that look. Uh oh.

"How did you know when you were in love JJ?" Jeanine's voice was serious. "My mother got all mushy and told me that I'd just know it, and there was nothing else in the world like it. When I meet the right guy, I'd feel it with all of my heart and soul." Jeanine dramatically put her hand over her heart and thumped.

"Do you think he's the right guy?" JJ asked.

Jeanine shrugged. "I know who the wrong guys are." She paused deep in thought. "Oh, JJ don't tell Bobby or Ga…" she stopped before she mentioned his name again. Whenever his name popped up in conversation JJ dipped her head as if to shut it out.

"I won't. Some things big brothers are better off not knowing about. I thought he'd have a canary when I told him what I did." Jill took another sip of her wine, and placed her glass next to the two empty bottles.

"He's mad that you can wield power tools like a pro?" Jeanine finished her glass, and took a bite of cold pizza. "Typical."

"No, not that. You know, in Afghanistan." It occurred to Jill just a little late, that Jeanine had no idea what she was talking about and she shouldn't know about that part of her life. Her brain scrambled to find a cover story.

"You went to Afghanistan?"

"I also went to Ireland and Paris, and I've seen the pyramids." She hoped Jeanine bought it, her tongue was becoming way too loose for comfort, and that thought brought on a wave of sadness. She didn't want to lie to Jeanine.

"He told me you traveled a lot. It sounds so exciting; can I see some of your pictures? I know you took pictures when you went, you'd never go anywhere without your camera."

"Sure, just not tonight ok?" Jill stood up and watched the room spin beneath her feet. She wasn't used to drinking this much, but it appeared Jeanine might be, she caught her arm, and laughed out loud.

"If you just stay sitting, that doesn't happen." Both women laughed so hard they tumbled onto the couch. "It's changing altitude that does it."

"I haven't gotten drunk in a long time." Jill snorted. "Well if you don't count the fourth of July, but before that it was about five or six years." She giggled.

The sound of tinkling bells floated through the air. Jeanine jumped. "That's my cell! Maybe it's Brent!"

Jill tried to focus on the pendulum clock on the wall, it couldn't be right. It read twelve thirty!

"Oh, hi." Judging by Jeanine's response, it must not be her Brent. "Well, I had to dig it out, it…no! I am not drunk! Either is JJ. Yup ok, I know, I know. I will, good bye Robert."

Jill refocused her eyes on Jeanine. "He always call you at this hour?"

"Only when he wants to be a pain in the ass, which lately is a lot." She giggled. "I've paid him back though, and interrupted a few of his evenings. Payback's a bitch."

Jill laughed. "You paid way too much attention when you were younger didn't you?"

"Learned from a pro. I think there's one more bottle of wine, I'll get it." Jeanine stood and braced herself with the back of the sofa. "It's raining again. Oh Stormy, I almost forgot.

"Stormy? You still have Stormy? Here?"

"Yep, she's on the porch, wet and pissed as all hell. I better let her in or she'll rip a hole in my pillow again when she goes in my room." Jeanine opened the front door and a gush of wind blew in, with it, a dark gray cat with yellow eyes skidded across the floor before composing itself to strut past Jill. The cat all but shot daggers at Jeanine. She glanced JJ's way but headed straight for the kitchen. Jeanine followed her, and reappeared a minute later with another bottle of wine and a corkscrew.

"That cat hates my parents' house. She likes it here, I can't blame her." Jeanine worked the corkscrew into the top of the bottle. Almost on cue the cat swaggered out and wound its way around her legs purring loudly. "It must be all of that tofu and healthy crap my mother tries to give her, although she thought the home-grown catnip was great."

With great effort, the cork popped out. Both women looked for their lost glasses.

"The hell with it!" Jeanine took a slug from the bottle and handed it to JJ.

JJ took a big gulp, and wiped her lips with the back of her hand. "You know this is the best wine I've ever tasted."

"It's pretty old, I guess that makes it good, right?"

"Right." Jill took another gulp and looked at the label that was slightly out of focus. "Very right." Someone wasn't going to be happy that they'd raided the stash in the basement. And why on earth was there a wine stash like this in the basement?

Jill woke in her old bedroom. She didn't remember climbing the steps but she must have. She remembered letting her eyes close for just a few minutes settling on the couch downstairs while she and Jeanine were playing an abbreviated version of Truth or Dare. She'd just confessed something that made her feel giddy, and had brought Jeanine to tears.

She concentrated on the image of Jeanine smiling like the Cheshire cat while a tear slid down her cheek, what had she told her?

Jill remembered letting go and slipping into a haze after so many nights of little or no sleep. If the small clock on the nightstand was right it was one o'clock in the afternoon.

One o'clock in the afternoon? Why was it so gray? Where was Jeanine? She sat up quickly and was caught by two strong familiar arms.

Galen.

CHAPTER 6

The wind was howling, whipping rain and hail against her window. Each drop sounded like a machine gun going off next to her ear. She knew exactly what that sounded like, proving that she hadn't slipped into some kind of time warp that her alcohol soaked brain tried to convince her of moments earlier.

Galen left her room, but his scent lingered and stirred unwanted memories. He held her and settled her back down onto the pillows, and she'd allowed him to do it. She propped herself up now.

What was *he* doing here?

Jill concentrated despite her pounding headache. Jeanine was here last night. They were laughing and talking, and had some pizza and wine.

Too much wine.

Where was Jeanine? Jill closed her eyes and slid her legs over the side of the bed. She had no idea what was going on, but she wouldn't find out by staying in bed.

"Whoa, JJ where do you think you're headed?" Galen was standing in her doorway holding a cup of what she hoped was coffee. She stood still and waited until the room stopped spinning.

"I'm getting up, where's Jeanine?" She said and blew out a breath. She thought their last meeting wasn't under the best circumstances, this meeting certainly had even less going for it. She felt like hell and probably looked even worse.

"Her parents' house. She left earlier, before the storm really set in." Galen said with absolutely no emotion. He was staring at her though, and his scrutiny made her uneasy.

"Oh." Jill didn't want to ask the obvious, but when did a storm set in?

"I brought you some coffee." He held the steaming cup out for her, "It's hot JJ. You must have had some night. Maybe you should sit."

She thought her legs wouldn't hold her for another minute anyway so she sat back on the bed careful not to spill, then took a sip and closed her eyes. Images of the previous night popped in and out, some eluded her altogether. One snapshot flickered across her mind's eye.

Oh, no.

"You carried me up here?" Her eyes dragged up from the floor and met his. He nodded.

"You had Jeanine a little worried, but apparently, you were just really tired." *And you scared the shit out of me by sleeping for so long.* "She mentioned you've been having a tough time sleeping lately. Insomnia, again?"

"Sometimes, it's difficult to just shut down." She confessed. But he knew that, and he'd found a sure cure a long time ago. *Do not think about THAT!*

He watched her take small sips of his coffee, and his heart did a somersault. He was coming here to rid himself of her. But that was before he'd had five hours to watch her sleep and wonder if he was in her dreams the way she was in his.

Or did he cause her nightmares? The ones that made her toss and turn and cry out as if she was being pursued by a hungry pack of wolves?

She'd come close to falling off of the bed when she rolled over, kicking off the blankets as if they were shackles that held her. He moved her back to the center of the bed as gently as possible, and stroked her cheek until she slept again.

He wanted to wake her, hold her, comfort her, tell her it would all be ok, but he wasn't so sure that he wasn't the one she was running from in those nightmares.

In her fits of sleep, her shirt rode up, and he couldn't believe his eyes. JJ had a scar on her back, a huge ugly scar. He'd gently lifted the material higher to get a better look at the gash while she settled back into sleep and was horrified by what he saw. She'd either been operated on by a butcher, or was sliced by a knife, or maybe a bullet? It nearly brought him to tears last night. But more than that it made him furious.

Galen hadn't meant to sit at her bedside and watch her sleep, or fight the demons that haunted her, but once he'd lifted her off of that cold couch and she snuggled into his chest as if she'd found home, he had a hard time putting her down. And when he put her on the bed and covered her, his body refused to cooperate and walk away from her and the very same bed he'd made love to her in so many times, giving her his heart and soul. The bed he'd held her in, as she took him to heaven and back so long ago, looked like it had waited for their return.

He'd brushed his fingers over the scar on her back, wishing it away, wishing the pain it must have caused away. And wishing the cutting pain in his heart away.

She slept for two hours after that, leaving him to imagine the terrible things that could have caused such a mark, one worse than the other until he was madder than he thought possible.

He absently rubbed at his chest, he cared too much still, more than he wanted to and probably much more than he should. Emotions he thought died when she left him, surged through him again, consuming him like a fire. Concern tuned to anger, and jealousy to vengeance.

At one point, he vowed aloud to inflict death on the asshole that scarred her body, and so help him, he would find out how she'd been marked like that. Her lashes had fluttered when he voiced his oath, and he wanted to believe he saw the corners of her lips turn upward, but she was sleeping.

He moved soft wisps of hair that slid across her face and sifted the chestnut silk between his fingers.

She was real. And she was here with him by her side. Again.

JJ was perfection, with or without the scar. Through the old T-shirt she wore, he studied the way her body had changed in the years that separated them.

"Galen?"

He didn't realize he'd been staring at her. "I'm sorry JJ, I…"

This was it, it was time, he couldn't wait for the perfect time because it may never come, she was here now, and so was he. He had to talk to her, and he needed answers. The only question he could think of wasn't one of the thousands of questions that had rolled around in his head for years. It was a new one, an immediate one, one that he had to bite back his temper to ask.

"How did you get the scar on your back JJ?" He asked.

The cup froze halfway to her lips. She slowly reached over and put it on the nightstand, then studied the floor, only once raising her eyes to meet his.

"You can tell me it's none of my business JJ. You can tell me to go to hell. That I don't deserve an explanation about anything in your life, and you'd be right. But, I want you to know something while you debate what you're going to tell me. I was going to come up here and have a bonfire with all of your things, and my things, and anything that was left of us. I contemplated burning the whole house down. I wanted to get you out of my system once and for all, because God knows nothing else has worked." He stood and took a few steps away, then came back to face her. "No matter what I do, you're there, even when you're not really there. And because you're not really there…shit this isn't coming out right." He dragged his hand through his hair, and blew out a breath. "I got here last night, and I couldn't do it. I just…I miss you, and I never stopped caring about you, though God knows I tried."

JJ stared dumbfounded, she never in a million years expected him to say any of the things that were pouring out of his lips, and now, her heart was breaking all over again.

For him.

He was trying so hard to find the right words. He looked mad, and hurt, and tired, and his eyes told her he was telling her the truth.

"I know. I did the same. I came here for the same thing." She stood up and walked to the closet wobbling only once, and pulled the door open. "And then I saw this."

Galen stared at the closet full of photography equipment and the things he'd wanted her to have. Equipment he bought and paid for that sat idle in his former game room until it was boxed up and put away.

He laughed.

Oh, sure now the peace offering works, but where were you seven years ago to see it? Use it?

"This changed your mind about burning my things?" He shook his head in disbelief.

"I wasn't going to burn your things." She gripped the knob. "I was going to collect mine and go. Now thanks to you, I can't fit all of my things in my car."

"Sure you can, who says this is yours? You weren't here to claim it." He watched as fire leapt into her eyes, the cool woman who sat on the bed and answered him as if he were just some average Joe was gone.

"You told me not to come back." She said with a touch of annoyance.

"I also asked you not to leave. You listened to one request but not the other?"

"It wasn't a request, you gave me an ultimatum."

"And you made a choice. And. I. Was. Not. It." He said, punctuating each word with his finger into his chest.

"That wasn't the choice I made Galen, and you know it." She shot back at him.

"I could have given you everything you wanted JJ, everything." He stared at her as she stepped toward him, unsure whether standing his ground was the safest bet at the moment.

"Then, why didn't you?" She hissed at him. "I didn't want anything but you. Not all of this, or *things*. I wanted you. Your love and trust, and you couldn't give me that."

He stared at her. *She thought he didn't trust her?*

"I loved you. Of course, I trusted you, I trusted you more than I trusted myself."

"Not enough to let me go and make a career for myself, do something I loved, something I am good at. Something you could be proud of." She turned her back on him, those last words spilled out on their own in a choked sob, but they stunned him into silence.

Jill's head was throbbing. The storm outside was nothing compared to the storm in her room. Sleet pummeled the windows as if it would shatter the glass. Jill flinched, then balled her hands into fists of frustration.

Instinctively he moved to sooth her, running his hands up and down her stiffened shoulders and arms. When she didn't pull away he closed the gap between them, resting his chin atop her head.

"JJ, I was always proud of you. I was amazed at all of your talent. And everyday I learned about some new talent you had. Everything you did, you did well." *And I was afraid I'd lose you to the world when they found out what you could do, and then I did anyway.*

She winced as if he slapped her. *The one thing that meant more to me than anything else I failed miserably at.*

"I just wanted to be someone other than poor little JJ, that you had to take care of." She said.

"And that scared the shit out of me. But you were never just poor little JJ, and you know that." He spun her to face him, remembering all of the emotions he'd felt then, and the regret he'd felt later but wouldn't admit. "I shouldn't have said the things I did. I didn't know what else to do. I was scared JJ, and I thought that you…" He held his breath. He was knee deep in it now, so he might as well finish what he'd started. "I know this sounds crazy now, and makes what I said even more absurd. I thought that you might be pregnant JJ, you were late."

Her shoulders went stiff under his hands. "You remembered that?"

He smiled like an embarrassed little boy caught with his hand in the cookie jar.

"When you told me you were late, I was happy. I know it's crazy, we were so young, but I actually was hoping you were. Even after you left, I was hoping, I knew you'd never risk our baby like that." It hurt to admit he liked the idea of JJ carrying his child then, even now he was aching for her.

Oh God, Oh God, Oh God! She closed her eyes against the memory of holding her sweet little lifeless baby boy in her arms, her son.

Galen's son.

A loud clap of thunder slammed above.

"JJ are you ok?" She paled and looked like she'd seen a ghost. "I didn't mean that the way it probably sounded."

"No, it's ok." Big round eyes stared up at him.

"I wanted to keep you safe JJ, I just went about it all wrong."

The look on her face filled him with a need so strong he had to look away, or kiss her senseless and dig himself a deeper hole than the one he was inching his way out of now.

Galen was beginning to see the light again, feel again, because for the few brief hours he'd spent with her, he felt alive. He silently vowed to himself that she'd be in his life again come hell or high water. He made a mistake before and lost her. He wouldn't do it again if she gave him a chance. He'd find a way.

This time she was going to chose him, but he wasn't giving her ultimatums or seven years to do it. No one else stirred the burning need inside him the way she did.

JJ was the air he breathed, and the water he drank to go on living. Why the hell hadn't he realized it sooner? He'd been thirsty and suffocating for too long.

"You weren't all wrong Galen. We both made mistakes." She sat on the edge of the bed because the weight she still carried was getting too heavy to bear.

"But maybe it's time we did this. Talked. We're not little kids anymore."

He sat next to her. The old mattress creaked and dipped, she slid into him. Color rose in her cheeks but she didn't move away.

Damn, she still blushed like she used to, which turned the heat building in his veins up another notch. JJ was still a perfect fit tucked under his arm. Galen cleared his throat.

"Still squeaks." It would take no effort to dip his head and taste those perfect lips, find that spot on her neck that made her giggle and melt in his arms. Lean her back and…

"So, does the floor." She stood, pushing off of his knee for leverage.

He captured her hand in his and held it, caressing her palm with his thumb while her eyes locked on his.

She was searching for something, but he wasn't sure what. A full minute passed before she blinked, moving her eyes to their joined hands. Her hand turned in his and she squeezed it tight then released him.

He stood on shaky legs, never noticing hers were doing the same.

"Maybe we should get something to eat." She said. "Is it me or does it look like we never left?"

He tucked his hands in his pockets to keep from touching her again. "There's a ton of food in the kitchen, and enough beer, wine and liquor to throw a frat party."

Galen's brows drew together. JJ's did the same.

"I have the feeling that the house isn't changing hands at all." Galen murmured.

"I was thinking the same thing." JJ said.

"You got the key from Bobby? He told you he sold it and closing was next week?"

"Uh huh."

"And that you left some things you might want here?" Galen asked.

"Yes. My old camera, and some personal things." Jill narrowed her eyes.

"Yea, me too." He didn't think it was a good idea to mention Jeanine's strange phone call at four in the morning just yet telling him she thought JJ was in trouble.

That call scared the shit out of him and had him scrambling to get across the Long Island Sound in record time. He'd deal with her later.

"Do you think he wanted us to be up here together?" Jill asked without expecting an answer.

Galen didn't have to think, he knew. How many times had Bobby asked him to find her, even to just talk to her? Then again, the sneaky rat had known all along where to find her.

"So, do you want to kill him?" Galen waited a beat. "Or thank him? I'm sort of torn between the two."

"We could thank him by sending him a bouquet of flowers with poison ivy twined between the stems. Seems to me, I recall him blowing up like a balloon when he gets near the stuff." JJ joked, then lowered her voice to a whisper. "Or maybe we could take him out to dinner sometime."

Was he feeling the same pull she did? She wasn't sure if it was for what they once had, or what seemed to be starting now. How could something be so difficult, yet so easy?

Galen caught the fact that she'd said 'we' when she talked about dinner.

"I say we do both." He was going to have a nice long talk with his friend Bobby soon. But right now, he had other things on his mind. This meeting was different than he ever imagined it would be, and he'd imagined quite a few scenarios. The woman he saw now was more confident than the JJ he knew, and it made her even more attractive.

She did seem awfully glad to be talking about something other than the past, or the now, and them. He watched her walk across the room as the T-shirt skimmed high on her thighs, he sucked in a breath, then narrowed his eyes.

"JJ. You never answered my original question."

"I think I'd like to eat something light, toast maybe?" If she didn't glance at him, he would have thought she was speaking to herself. "After I take a shower and a few aspirin." She spun to face him, and the room held steady this time. "Speaking of light, it's awfully dark." She flipped the wall switch and waited. Nothing.

"I guess we're in the dark for now. Power lines are probably down with all of this wind and rain." He answered absently; somewhere in his head he knew that only mere seconds ago, something seemed very important. He'd think about it all in a bit. Right now a mile of leg was distracting him. Galen silently thanked the powers that be for all of the possibilities presented to him here and now. "I'll get a few candles, it'll be roma…nice." Had he really been about to utter the word romantic?

"It's ok, I can shower in the dark." Jill gathered some clothes and headed for the hall bathroom. Galen nearly groaned when she bent over to reach for whatever the hell it was she dropped.

Rain and hail pounded the roof above. He stepped out of her room to give himself some space, and looked over at the dark bathroom.

"There's probably no hot water." He noted. Not that there ever was a lot of hot water, unless Bobby had replaced the old boiler recently.

"It's ok, I've bathed in worse conditions." She answered without thinking and cringed after she caught his baffled look. "The plumbing in my house is temperamental."

"Isn't it dangerous to take a shower in a thunder storm?" Galen asked while inadvertently blocking her path to the bathroom. "I think I read that somewhere."

Jill rolled her eyes.

"It's also dangerous to keep a woman with a hangover from getting to the shower and aspirin. I'm willing to take my chances that I'll be fine in the shower, are you willing to chance spending the rest of the day with a stinky woman who has a killer headache?"

His brain took another left turn. She was headed for the same bathroom shower that he'd been just about positive that they'd conceived a child in. They'd been too caught up in each other to use protection.

"I was sort of hoping to take that shower with what little daylight is left. Galen?" She asked with a confused look.

Oh, hell he was going to need a shower if he kept traveling down this little section of memory lane.

The next clap of thunder cleared his head. "I'll get some candles, and see what I can find for lunch."

Galen walked down the narrow steps slowly, it was going to be a rough day and night if this storm kept up, but it was also going to give him an opportunity to be with her.

There was still so much they'd left unsaid and unfinished, but this was a start.

Galen snorted. A start. He'd wanted an end.

He poked apart the curtains on the front door's window, it was raining and hailing as if a plague had descended on the town. If he didn't move JJ's car into the driveway, it was going to float away in the rapidly rising water that made the narrow street look more like a stream.

He was surprised he hadn't floated away with his neighbor's pick up truck while on the ferry this morning.

After the phone call that woke him at four in the morning, he was nearly frantic when his car didn't start. He thanked God for Henry Reese and his pick-up truck. The older man had been up walking his dog and heard Galen's plea for the car to start, then offered him the use his truck when Galen explained his emergency. The ferry had pitched and rocked so badly that for a while he thought he might have to swim to Connecticut. The boat that crossed the sound at six this morning was the single boat that left the dock. All other trips had been cancelled due to the nor'easter that was raining hell on them now.

Glass Elevators

Galen lit the jar candle that said pumpkin pie on the label, then dug through a drawer in the china cabinet to find two smaller versions of what he guessed was the same scent. They looked like they were the same color.

He found JJ's keys next to her bag on the table. Her wallet hit the floor when he pulled the key chain from under it. Picking it up, he noticed her Pennsylvania driver's license.

So, that's where she lives, and she used her full name. Jillian Jayne LeBuntoski.

It was the first time he'd seen her name written out in a long time.

A card slipped out of one of the side pockets, he picked it up and pushed it back in, then quickly pulled it back out. It was from the *I Did it Myself* chain of craft stores, and had some sort of note about colors hand written on the back of it. According to the title beneath the made up name Jillian Leigh, she really was in the upper tier of management of the growing company.

Another small card was written in a foreign language, some of the writing looked like hieroglyphics to him.

Galen put the wallet and card back on the table and headed out the door stepping over his own gym bag that he left on the porch. It was wet, probably soaked through. The roof hadn't provided much of a buffer against the horizontal rain and sleet still coming from the south. If he judged it right, this storm had a long way to go. As he stepped off the porch, the rain mixed with snow.

CHAPTER 7

Bobby had no way of knowing for sure whether or not Mac had made it up to the house. There had been only one ferry out, and he was supposed to be on it. One of the ferry employees told him that she thought she saw him board. He wasn't answering his phone at the beach house, and there was no service on his cell.

The damned storm had cut his call with Jeanine short, but he was almost certain she said he was there. He also thought Jeanine said something about JJ and wine. He couldn't be sure, but Jeanine sounded happy on the phone. He had no way to call her back to be sure.

The northeast coast from New Jersey to Maine was being battered by a huge storm. A Nor'easter they kept calling it. Judging from the way the rain was beating at his window, it was going to be a while before he would know anything about the success or failure of his plan.

It was the middle of the day, and it looked as dark as night. The weather reports said that parts of New England were getting hail and ice, and in some places snow. Wouldn't that be a kick? If Mac had made it to the house, and was still there with JJ, who knows what could happen? If they didn't kill each other first, they just might be thanking him sometime in the near future.

They might do quite a bit of fighting at first, and maybe that's just what they needed to clear the air, and maybe even start over.

He'd done what he could for two people who meant everything to him. He should have done something sooner. But like JJ used to say, everything happens for a reason, sometimes it just takes a while to figure that reason out.

Jeanine sat in her old room and stared out the window, the book she was reading hung limply from her hand. Galen had arrived just as Bobby hoped he would, and judging from what she'd seen, he still loved JJ. The concern in his eyes was evident as he carried her up the stairs to her room. As a matter of fact, it was all very romantic. She only felt a little bit guilty about her part in Bobby's so called plan B. She wondered what the heck plan A was, and how many plans the idiot had up his sleeve. She hated deceiving people she cared about, but maybe it was ok if everything worked out in the end.

When Galen sent her home, and told her he'd take care of JJ, the guilt faded a bit. When she saw him sitting at the end of JJ's bed and watching over her as she slept, Jeanine realized that her dumbass brother had finally done something really good.

How many men would venture out into a storm and sit with the woman they lost years ago just to make sure that she was ok? Granted she made up a story about JJ being really depressed and saying some crazy things to get Galen's attention, she'd worry about that later.

She wondered if Brent would worry about her like that? He called and left four voicemails for her since last night. If this damned storm didn't blow in when it did, she might be snuggled in his arms now. Instead Jeanine was raiding her secret chocolate stash, and reading a romance novel in which the heroin was currently being held firmly in her lover's strong embrace while he tortured her with demanding lips and a probing tongue.

She broke off another piece of chocolate defiantly. If her mother thought that carob bars could replace rich creamy chocolate, the woman was dreaming. None of the food that was "natural" and 'good for you' ever tasted like this.

Maybe initially some of her mom's rabbit food was ok, but sometimes the aftertaste would linger until the only thing that chased it was a good strong mouthwash, the kind that could peel wallpaper off the wall and kill ninety nine percent of every germ known to mankind.

She popped a rectangle of chocolate bearing the letter r into her mouth. She figured she'd emerge from her room after she'd finished off the s-h-e and y sections.

Bobby owed her big time, this moving home for a few days was putting a damper on her life. But if it meant that JJ would be happy, she'd gladly suffer. She just wouldn't let Bobby know that.

Jeanine wasn't convinced that JJ and Galen would buy the story about the house sale. In fact, she'd slipped so many times that JJ must have seen through the scheme. All JJ and Galen had to do was talk to one another and they'd probably figure out that her well-meaning brother had played matchmaker, or re-matchmaker.

If they talked to one another without throwing things or strangling each other, they stood a chance. And even if it didn't work out, they would hopefully settle something so that they could all be in the same room with one another again.

Judging from Galen's mood when he told her she should get home before the storm got worse, and the concern he showed for someone he had proclaimed was history, and JJ's last coherent statements that she was still deeply and irrevocably in love with Galen, the two needed this time together. They had hurdles to get over, and Jeanine hoped they'd at least step up to the starting line and try again. The phone call she made last night might have made all the difference. Galen certainly showed up in a hurry. She just hoped JJ would forgive her for it.

The wind whipped at her bedroom window, and she turned to look.

"Holy cow, it's snowing!" She bounded off of the bed and moved the curtains aside for a better look. It was snowing and thundering, how bizarre? But hadn't the past twenty-four hours been just a little bizarre?

"You just never know." She whispered.

The shower felt great. There was some hot water left in the pipes, but Jill didn't linger, maybe Galen would want a shower too, and he wasn't fond of cold showers. Jill wrapped herself in a towel and untangled her wet tresses. Either the aspirin had kicked in fast, or the shower had worked wonders, because she felt good, energized. Like she did just before leaving for a new project.

A loud crash of thunder seemed to slam into the roof of the house just above her head, she flinched then cursed under her breath and reminded herself that it was only thunder. Curiosity had her parting the curtains and peeking out the window. Her car was moving up the driveway. In her view from the small bathroom window she could see that the road had become a river, and the rain had turned to...was that snow?

Galen must be moving the car for her. It was hard to be mad when he was being so considerate. She watched her car until it was bumper to bumper with what she supposed was Galen's rusty old pick-up truck? Maybe he liked old trucks. He climbed out of her car and locked it, then shot a glance at the window she was peering out of as if he felt her gaze. She wrapped the towel tighter and promised herself that she would get her emotions and her rebellious body under control.

Galen dragged his soggy gym bag in from the porch and deposited it at the bottom of the steps. When he looked up he was surprised to see JJ dressed in a pair of jeans and a flannel shirt, coming down. Her feet were bare, and her toes wriggled as she spoke to him.

"I think there's some warm water left. You should get out of those wet things and…Galen?" She ducked her head trying to meet his eyes.

Galen was couldn't believe what he was seeing, he didn't mean to stare but his eyes wouldn't budge from her toes. The second toe of her left foot to be exact. On it she wore a ring that bore a remarkable resemblance to the opal he'd once given her. She looked down and caught sight of his waterlogged bag.

"Your things got wet, do you have anything else? Another bag?" She stepped down the last step, and reached for the bag. "I'll see if there's something that didn't get too soaked in here, you go take a shower with what warm water that's left."

Did the woman have a clue how sexy she looked standing there in those tight jeans, and green plaid shirt? Her damp hair draped like a satin curtain down her back, her face clean and fresh, and those big green eyes smiling at him, tempting him, like the little opal that winked on her toe. She was still wearing his ring. Did she know what it was? Or had it become just some piece of jewelry she happened to put on like the earrings that were caressing her neck each time she moved her head?

Jill shivered, her bare feet hit a patch of cold water on the floor, and she slid. Galen steadied her before her feet went out from under her. His bag hit the wooden floor with a thud.

"Oh!" Jill grabbed his arm.

He had her in his arms, and it was too much for either of them to ignore. Slowly, without taking his eyes away from hers, he dipped his head and brushed his lips against hers. Her hands slid up over his shoulders and around his neck as she pressed against him. He pulled her in when she sighed his name.

Damp cold became moist heat between them. He lifted her to the steps and put her down, unwilling to make the long trek up. It had been too long since he'd wanted… no, needed something so badly. She dropped her hands beneath his shirt and lifted it over his head. A tiny voice inside of her told her she was crazy, she ignored it and ran her fingers over solid muscle that quivered beneath her fingers.

It had been so long since she'd felt the warmth of him over her, around her, in her. She wanted him, and yes, she needed him now. No matter how insane it was, she needed him.

"I want you more than I want my next breath JJ." His mouth lowered to hers. She pulled him down and lifted herself to him.

She could hardly breathe for wanting him. As he pulled her hips close and sank into her softness the world melted away and there was only the two of them left. He moved slowly at first, and filled her more with each thrust. She locked her legs around him pulling him deeper inside until she felt like he reached the core of her existence, linking their bodies and souls again.

Mine! The thought raced through his mind in a roar.

"Open your eyes JJ, don't leave me now." He crushed his mouth to hers as they shattered together in each other's arms.

Neither wanted to think, or talk. Afraid of what might be said, and what might not be said. His fingers skimmed the scar on her back. He'd wait to ask about it, but he would find out who had marred her perfect skin, then make whoever it was pay.

Jill lifted her head off of his chest when his heart rate picked up again after it had slowed to a steady thrum. His fingers were tracing a line up her back, and it felt wonderful. The stairway was a brighter than it had been earlier, and now, over her bare skin she felt a cool breeze. She sat up.

"Snow."

Galen lifted his head. It wasn't exactly what he expected her to say. "Snow?"

She nodded. "Snow, it looks like a blizzard."

She looked directly out the door's window where the curtain had parted, probably when Galen had come in and shut the door. He sat up to look. Sure enough it looked as if there was already a thick coating on branches and railings, and a few inches blanketing the ground. The road looked like a river running through the snow-covered woods. The snow was blowing horizontally in gusts. JJ shivered beside him, he draped his arm around her and kissed her temple.

I love you.

Three words made his lips tingle. Three little words he hadn't said for a long time wanted to escape, but he wouldn't allow those words to be said. Not now, it would be like putting a nail in his own coffin.

As his lips brushed her temple, warmth pooled in her belly again. She snuggled close under his protective arm. They sat in silence on the steps for a few moments; it felt right to be there, together again. There was so much she wanted to tell him, so much she wanted to share with him, she just wasn't sure he was feeling the same, or that he'd want to hear what she had to say.

He watched JJ's eyes close, a shiver ran through her again. He rubbed her shoulders and reached for her shirt draping it over her. "You're cold. I'll get some of that wood that's under the tarp and build a fire." He rose and grabbed his sweat pants, stepping into them as he spoke.

"Whooo, that's cold and wet." He gingerly stepped back out of the icy sweats.

JJ laughed at his comical reaction, then held her shirt out for him, and hugged herself for warmth.

"It is getting cold in here. I think I can dig something up to put on. I wouldn't want to give old Mrs. Schumacher an eyeful." He walked up the steps on wobbly legs, determined that she wouldn't notice. Two minutes later he was back down the stairs, dressed in another pair of gray sweats. He approached her from behind as she fastened a button on her shirt. She was staring out the window and seemed to be miles away.

He gently laid his hands on her shoulders, and kissed the top of her head. Her hands reached up to cover his. This was what she wanted, what she dreamed of, yet it all seemed surreal. Thunder crashed overhead again.

"Don't think too much JJ." He said.

She was afraid that she hadn't been thinking at all, and neither was he.

"I'll see what I can find in the kitchen, maybe make some coffee or tea or...something." She needed a little space, and time to sort out what just happened. Maybe he was right and she should just let it be and not think too much.

What was that saying? 'People who don't learn from their mistakes are doomed to repeat them.' It nagged her while she stirred a pot of canned soup over the gas burner. She'd come back to move on, and found herself in the same spot she was in seven years earlier.

After the storm let up they would certainly go their separate ways. Maybe they'd part as friends, or maybe not. But one thing was certain; Galen had awakened needs that she'd forgotten could be so wonderful, and powerful. There was still so much they hadn't spoken of, old wounds that needed tending. This was the opportunity she'd wanted for so long, and she knew she had to make use of this time no matter how they'd been brought together. It was now or possibly never, and *never* just didn't work anymore.

They sat at the kitchen table lit with tapered candles. He'd brought her a sweater to throw on over the flannel shirt for warmth. She hadn't said much since he sat down across from her. The silence was too much. Even with the wind whipping at the door and rattling old windows the silence between them screamed for relief.

"I…" Both spoke at once, and stopped waiting for the other to begin.

When she stared for a moment, Galen began again. "JJ, I know we just jumped into this, but if you're thinking that what we did didn't mean anything to me, you're wrong."

Her eyes closed briefly and her face relaxed into a half smile before she continued to sip chicken and stars soup off of a large rounded spoon. She held the spoon up as if she'd made a decision and was going to use it as a prop. The spoon batted the air a few times before she settled on her next words, then she used it like a conductor in front of his assembled orchestra. She started and stopped two or three times before she completed a sentence.

"I…well, Galen…thank you. For that. It meant… I…" JJ blew out a breath ruffling her hair. She could do this, what happened to her voice? Her composure? Her resolve? Around Galen it all seemed to come and go with no rhyme or reason. She couldn't let that happen, again. She cleared her throat and realized that she'd been waving her soup spoon around like a baton. She deliberately placed it down then rearranged it twice. She glanced up to see Galen watching her intently if not with a bit of amusement in his eyes. "There's so much that you don't know about me. I'm not in the habit of jumping into bed with just anyone. And, I never thought that we… I'm not…that is…"

Her little admission had his heart singing and brought a genuine smile to his face. Her eyes met his briefly then they danced around the room and studied the bowl of soup as if it held the answers to the mysteries of the world. If he wasn't mistaken, she was trying to *not say* as much as she was trying to say. "We never made it to the bed to jump in it."

JJ stopped fumbling and babbling, and this time when their eyes met, hers were smiling, though she didn't want them to be. "You know what I mean. What I'm trying to tell you…oh the hell with it. Galen, we didn't use any protection, I'm not on the pill, and unless you've visited the doctor for a…" she made a snipping motion that caused him to wince, "or had some kind of magic condom…"

His heart skipped a beat or ten as the impact of what she was finally saying sank in. He swallowed hard.

"I didn't think so." She picked up her bowl and brought it to the sink dumping the remaining contents. Only once before had they made love without protection, and that once had been all it took. She really hadn't moved far from her past at all.

"JJ I'm sorry, it was, it just happened. I thought that you…" He felt like a bumbling teen. "Geez, JJ." He stood and held her. What was he thinking? He'd never been so careless except for that once with her so long ago.

"It's not your fault Galen, I should have stopped, should have thought about consequences. But the truth is I didn't want to stop, and that's not on you, it's me. I wasn't thinking at all." She said.

"Don't do that, I should have been the one to think, but when I'm around you…when I carried you upstairs last night I wanted you. I wanted to lie in that bed next to you and make love to you, then make promises and plans. It was as if the past seven years didn't happen. So don't protect me JJ. If you wind up…" he stopped and started three times before he muttered a curse then did exactly as she had and spit out what he wanted to say, "If something has begun here, I'll see it through to whatever end you choose."

"I'm not a little girl who can't take care of herself."

"I didn't say you were." He watched her struggle for composure that came and went with each passing breath.

She moved around him, "Why is it that I feel like I'm dancing around a big wall when what I really want to do is talk to you?" She stopped and stared at him shaking her head. "None of this has gone the way I thought it would. There's so much I have to tell you, so much I want to know about you and…" Her voice trailed off again and she looked away, then stared at him as if she was looking at a stranger. "But…I'm not sure who I'm talking to."

He folded his arms in front of his chest to keep from reaching out and pulling her to him. "What does that mean?"

"It means that I thought I knew you, then I didn't… know you. I've watched you, read the stories, heard the rumors about you. I never really wanted to believe any of it, even when it was all there, always there. I thought of THAT guy as someone I never knew, not the man I once lo..." She stopped herself, and recomposed her thoughts. "I saw you at the hotel…in the elevator with two women draped around you, I don't know that man." She took a breath. "Then I came here, and you made it hard to forget that so much time has passed."

He watched her rinse out her bowl and the pot she'd heated the soup in, knowing that keeping her hands busy helped her to think. She shut the water off and turned to face him fully. "So, what I want to know is, who are you Galen? Who are you really? That guy I saw in the elevator? The guy the tabloids love and can't get enough of? Or the man who dropped everything and came here, then carried me upstairs and sat watching me sleep because he thought there was something wrong?" She swallowed hard. "I'm having a hard time putting those two people in the same body."

He rubbed a rut in his forehead. Hell there were times he wasn't sure who he was.

"I made mistakes, more than my share of them. Oh hell, tons of them." He began, and stopped just as she had, but he knew she wanted no less than the truth from him. "Sometimes I'm not sure who I am, lately it's been even more confusing." He watched her carefully, when she didn't look like she was going to smack him or bolt from the room, he continued. "The biggest mistake I could make now would be to ignore this, what's here between us now."

"You don't really know who I am anymore Galen. There's so much…"

"I don't want a confession from you JJ, I don't think you want any confessions from me either. But I'd really like to get past the crap that created the wall you keep dancing behind that's between us, then see if we can go somewhere from there."

"That *crap* is a lifetime. We knew each other once upon a time, and I think what we just did was a part of that." She turned the cold water back on and ran her hands under the stream then abruptly turned it off and reached for a towel. "I made love with the man I knew seven years ago, and you made the woman you once knew sail to heaven again. But we don't really know each other at all *Mac*, not anymore."

The name Mac was like a slap in the face coming from her, and it stung. He closed his eyes because she was right. Time had marched on, stomped on and smashed all in its way without regard to what once was. What did he know about her now? The woman his JJ had become was a mystery.

But he knew what he felt, what his gut was telling him. The fact that he had feelings again was a major step in the right direction, even if it meant he might be crushed again. He knew what it was like to have nothing inside, to go through the motions, living up to someone else's idea of what he should be, he wasn't going back there. Not without a fight. This older, daring, more confident JJ was more than he could have imagined, she'd built on perfection and was even more wonderful now. If the initial attraction was a memory trip, what he saw and wanted now wasn't. She was real, not a clone. Not perfect, but as close to his idea of perfection as he could imagine. She was unique and special and all he ever wanted.

"Galen. Not Mac, never Mac to you JJ." He corrected her. "And considering what I'm feeling now, and the fact that I'm feeling at all, I think we should probably get around that wall." He waited a beat to see her reaction. When her eyes lit, he pushed her a little more out of her comfort zone, and stepped toward her. "Just in case we want to dance again." Mischief lit his eyes as he took her hand and spun her around in the small kitchen so that she wound up nestled firmly against his chest, then he swayed back and forth without music.

"Galen McInnes I'm trying to be serious." And she *was*. But just then, she couldn't help herself, and she started laughing, and swaying with him. He was crazy, he'd gone nuts, absolutely insane, and Bobby had neglected to tell her. Insanity might just define this whole episode.

He whispered in her ear as they continued to sway. "That you are, so we'll be serious." He lead her back to the table and pulled out a chair gesturing for her to sit, then pulled another ladder back chair away from the table and sat on it backwards resting his chin on his folded arms across the back of the chair. "Tell me about yourself JJ. What have you been doing for the past seven years?"

"You're insane aren't you?" She bit back a laugh, and resisted touching the spot on her neck where his breath had cause goose bumps to rise.

"Could be. Sometimes I'm not sure." He waited for her to answer his question, and when she looked like there was a filibuster going on inside that pretty little head of hers, he figured he'd help her out. By the time she arranged whatever it was she wanted to say without hurting his feelings, or saying what she really wanted to say, the storm could be over.

He cleared his throat. "Let me take a stab at this?" He didn't wait for an answer. "Picture this, a very accomplished businesswoman…a regular retail giant…returns to her roots, the house she'd left long ago. She's met by her well meaning, but conniving friend that she treated like a sister, who convinces her to stay by lulling her into a false sense of security with alcohol. A storm brews outside. She's trapped in the old house, no contact with the outside world, if you don't count Mrs. Schumacher, who's probably pinned her front drapes back for an even better view of the stairs now. The wind is howling, snow is falling…it's a blizzard. And a psychotic baseball player who watched strike three pass for the last out of game seven of the world series…so you know he's not a happy camper, appears in her bedroom after her night of wild drinking and partying…"

Glass Elevators

"I'm not a retail giant. It was not wild drinking, and there was no party."

"Not according to Jeanine." He smirked and continued. "This is my story you'll have a chance later. The famous baseball player has spent the last few years miserable, everyone around him thought differently, they though he was funny, and daring, and had it all. He drank too much, partied it up and did some pretty outrageous things. But nothing made him happy; not five homerun titles, not three World Series rings, cars, money, nothing. Because of something that happened a long time ago, he's got a chip on his shoulder the size of Mount Everest, and it's heavy. He blames anyone and everyone for his misery, while pretending to be normal." At her questioning look he rescinded the last statement. "Ok, maybe not so normal. He's prepared to do whatever it takes to rid himself of the chip, and the misery. The phone rings in the middle of the night, and he gets his chance. He stands over his nemesis watching her sleep, mad as all hell that he was called to rescue her from the depths of despair she'd spiraled into-according to that wonderful friend. He's mad about things that happened ages ago and he couldn't let go of. And little by little as he watches her in the midst of fitful dreams and peaceful sleep, the ugly mad baseball player realizes that he still cares about her, and would have swam the Sound to help her. The question that haunted him through the night is why? Then he held her, and knew. People grow, they change, but they're always who they started out to be underneath it all. They make mistakes and learn, and make adjustments. And as I'm sitting here, making a complete fool of myself…I bet you missed my stories just a little? I still see the JJ I knew and loved, and I see more. I want to get to know the more, the woman I missed seeing her become. And I'm really hoping that this is going to be one of those stories that ends with an ever after that's happy."

She blinked at him, not sure she'd heard him right, but amused all the same. How could she forget the stories he told? The boy short on words for everyday conversation loved his stories, and loved telling them to her. He could make the bland everyday grind sound like an adventure whenever he thought she needed cheering up.

"JJ?" He asked in a whisper when he stood and approached her. "There's only one thing I really need to know about you now, right now. Is there someone else in your life?"

Jill shifted, she could lie, but what was the sense? He wanted to talk, he wanted to know about her, and she had been so willing to tell him and show him how successful she'd become without him, now she couldn't think. She couldn't put together a coherent sentence. She shook her head slowly.

"No Galen, there is no one else." The simple admission left her open and vulnerable, and uncomfortable. The kitchen was suddenly very small, and the winds that whipped snow against the window howled loud. "There's really never been anyone else." She gasped at her admission, but it was too late to take it back.

His smile beamed. "So there's hope for me. We're stuck here together JJ, it doesn't look as though the storm is letting up anytime soon. We have nothing but time now. It seems to me we could get to know each other again. And I would like nothing better than to get to know you again JJ…or should I call you Jillian Leigh?"

She took her time answering him as usual.

"JJ please. But Galen, I don't think you're going to like who you'll meet, sometimes I don't like her." She said.

Her admission made him flinch, but he caught himself and pressed on. "Why don't you let me be the judge of that? Trust me JJ. I'm not too fond of the guy I've become lately either."

CHAPTER 8

Somewhere in the recesses of her mind 'trust me' played like an old record skipping on a scratch. She'd done that once and where did it land her?

Alone.

Alone in a remote hospital thousands of miles away in Lebanon on New Year's Eve, delivering Galen's stillborn son. A son he never knew about.

She watched reruns months later on some cable channel of the show 'Wild and Single" that was doing a New Year's special, he'd been all over some buxom blonde on the beach of a Caribbean resort just about the time JJ was handing her sweet lifeless baby back to the nurse.

"I'm not who you think I am." She began.

"Then tell me JJ. You have a big advantage here, you know all about me, and I'm sure it's more than I wish you knew. I'm not proud of a lot of things, but I can't go back and change the past. I can be here with you now, and we can learn about each other, or do what we've wasted too much time doing, ignoring each other." He took a breath and shook his head. "You are a very successful business woman from what I understand, managing a chain of hobby stores?"

"*I Did It Myself*, crafts, art, and hobbies. We're starting a line of scale model doll houses." She smiled. "That's part of why I was in Manhattan this past week. But, if I'm going to be totally honest, I'm not just managing the stores Galen, they're mine. I have a friend of mine play the role of CEO, and it's her face out there for the public to see, but, it's all mine. I just like the anonymity, not being in the spotlight."

He was silent for a moment, then seemed to digest what she'd said and grinned.

"Now was that so hard?" He reached for her hand, and she let him take it. "Let's go by the fireplace, it'll be warmer there. You look like you're cold."

She was cold, none of what she was about to tell him fit the warm and fuzzy category. She followed him through the kitchen door and sat on the couch opposite the fireplace; he tossed a log on the fire and settled on the floor next to the couch.

"You still take pictures I noticed." He stared into the fireplace watching the flames lick at the new log he'd fed it. "You always had a good eye. I still have some of the pictures you took of us. Bobby does too."

"I know he told me." She paused and figured that she might as well dive in head first. His shoulder brushed her knee, it would be so easy to slide down next to him and snuggle under his arm. The warmth of his touch swept her into the moment and gave her courage, which she knew was silly, but ran with it. "Did you ever hear of PJ Storm?"

"Who hasn't? The guy has guts. I read the article and saw the pictures he shot in Africa. Then the stuff in Egypt... those pictures from Iraq were intense too. And that stuff he just did from Afghanistan and Syria, unbelievable." He smiled. "He's good. You met him? Rumor has it no one knows what he looks like."

"Why do you think PJ Storm is a man?"

"PJ Storm has to be a guy. To get to the places he's been, get the shots he's taken. Even news crews can't get the stuff he does."

Jill smiled. "Galen, you're not the only one who's changed their name."

He turned and stared at her. "I saw JJ, you use the name Jillian Leigh."

"Sometimes." She cocked her head to the side and nodded.

"I did the same, it's not a crime." He turned to face her and rested his arm over her knees. "I'm guessing short for Le Buntonski?"

She nodded.

"So you think PJ Storm is a good photographer? And a decent writer? And obviously, a man?" JJ asked.

"You know him, you've met him? Her? Is he a she?" Galen asked.

"You've met her too Galen." She bit her lips together waiting for it to sink in. He went very still for a moment, then pulled away. His breathing became labored and his face was growing paler by the minute. "Galen…"

"Don't." His hands few up to ward off her touch as he stood to face her. "NO! Don't you dare tall me what I think you're about to say."

She stood to meet him eye to eye. He stared at her for an eon, and she thought she saw crazed anger in his eyes just before he slammed them shut. A moment later he opened them and glared at her the way he had when she told him she was leaving.

"Are you out of your fucking mind? Do you have a damned death wish JJ?"

"What happened to he's good? He's got guts?" She asked.

"That was before he was you!" He paced. "No wonder I couldn't find you, you were all over the world 'taking pictures with a conscience', isn't that what they say about him…you? Oh, shit…I can't believe this."

"I do what I think is right, expose what people should see."

"And standing nose to nose with that highjacker was right?" He spun on her, a litany of pictures he'd seen credited to PJ Storm fast forwarded through his head. "Holy crap, that famine, the pictures from Iraq, and that asshole dictator…"

"It's what I do Galen. And I do it well." She cut him off before he could go on. "I used a special lens, I wasn't nose to nose with anyone, he never even knew I was there."

"There's a damned price on your head." His tone slid into a depth she'd never heard from him before.

"I'm well aware of the threats, that's why not many people know what you do now. And why I keep a low profile with *I Did It Myself.* I'm seen just enough so that no one would ever put my careers together."

He stared at her as the seriousness of what she'd just divulged set in and gutted him. "Bobby knows."

She nodded. "He doesn't like it much either. But, it's how I got to be where I am today."

"Being shot at…to get pictures?"

"I don't get shot at all of the time."

He moved so quickly she didn't have time to react as he lifted her shirt to expose her back. "Someone didn't miss JJ."

"I made a mistake, and I paid for it. It's my life." She tugged her shirt back down.

"And is it worth so little?" He stared, willing her to admit what she did was crazy. She didn't budge, they stood nose to nose.

"I don't know Mac, is it much different than drinking yourself into a stupor every night, and once in a while just for kicks driving a Porsche into a tree, or into the nearest ditch after you survived the first crash and burn? You test air bags for the fun of it? Or were you on a mission?"

His eyes narrowed, she'd heard about his incidents. "It's not the same."

"Your damned right it's not, I'm making a living out there doing something worthwhile by exposing the injustices of the world. And you are just hell bent on wasting all of that God given talent you have by destroying your life." She poked him in the chest.

He threw his head back. "And you're saving the world, right?"

"NO, I'm not saving the world." JJ yelled back.

"You like being shot at then? You do have a death wish."

"I don't like being shot at, it scares the crap out of me." She blew out a breath. "You just learn to stop showing it."

He dragged a hand through his hair. "Why JJ? Why do you do it?"

She rubbed her arms that had suddenly gone cold. She answered him honestly. "For the same reason you dive head first into a base Galen, why you've suffered six concussions last I counted. Because I can, and I'm good at it, and up until I actually took a hit, I loved it. The thrill of it, the risk, and maybe somehow thinking I was doing something good in this messed up world. How does drinking yourself into oblivion get into the same category?"

He sat as if his knees couldn't support his weight anymore, hands clasped together in front of him, elbows resting on his knees.

"It doesn't. It was stupid. I was stupid." He looked over to her. "It's only five concussions counting the two in college. And it's still not the same."

"The drinking binges aren't the same Galen. That just makes me so sad, and so mad at you. I wanted to call. To yell, to pound some sense into you. I wished you would stop, so many times I hoped…" She stopped, and a wan smile pulled at her lips. He didn't need that lecture now. "The playing hard…we both take risks in our jobs. And we're both doing something we love." She sat next to him. "Would you give up playing because someone else thought it wasn't good for you?"

"Are you going to give up getting shot at?" He paused. "I didn't mean it like that."

She laughed. "Yes, you did Galen. And for what it's worth, I don't try to get shot at. I'm actually very good at blending in, I've got that *Plain Jane* thing going you know?"

His temper was leveling off. "You aren't a plain Jane."

"What do you think the PJ stands for?" She asked with a smile.

"So when is your next trip to a hell hole?" Now he wished he didn't know that guy with brass balls who kept half of the world's crazies wondering how they'd been exposed was in fact his JJ. JJ the sweet woman sitting next to him snuggling into an over sized flannel shirt that he'd all but torn off and made love to like there was no tomorrow.

"I'm not sure, I'm in the middle of something now in New York, but I may be headed for Columbia in two weeks."

"And now that I know, I'm supposed to sleep at night when you're out *working*?"

"Bobby does." She smiled. "I check in with him before and after. Otherwise I get a thousand messages, or he drives Stasha crazy. Stasha is my right arm, she's my assistant, and the face of my retail chain."

"That's fine for Bobby, Bobby didn't just make love to you." He said.

"I'll be fine Galen. I over reacted, it's just that…" She chose her words carefully, "…when I said there was no one now, there hasn't been anyone since…there's been no time, and I…"

His heart soared and broke with her shy smile. "You only know me."

She nodded, and he reached for her. "Geez JJ what did we do to each other?"

"Do you think we can be friends again?" She asked still pressed up against him.

He pulled back from their embrace. "I don't want to be friends again JJ, I want more."

"I won't give up who I am." She said.

"I made that mistake once, I won't ask you to. But it doesn't mean I have to like it." He said.

Saying that and living it were two different things. But she'd take him at his word for now.

"Thank you."

There was a long silence. The fire spit and crackled as the winds outside howled and whipped snow into a blinding white blanket, the two held on to each other as if their lives depended on the other's heart to beat. "Can I ask you a favor?" She said.

"Anything."

JJ knew what she was going to ask had to be his decision, but maybe she could put a seed in his head.

"Could you not test you liver so frequently? And I'd really appreciate it if you didn't drive afterward either. Can you promise me you won't drive like that anymore?"

He looked down into her pleading eyes and made himself a promise he hoped he could keep. "I think I can give that a shot. I think maybe I need to…you know, take a break from a few things."

"I'll do whatever I can to help." She offered.

"You have no idea what you've already done." He smiled down at her and her heart melted again. "You have to promise me something too JJ?"

"Galen…"

"Just promise me that you'll at least consider taking pictures of puppies and bunnies and babies with drool? There's a big market for those. Hey what about taking pictures of your favorite athlete in action?" He smiled a cheesy grin. "I pay well."

She nodded into his shoulder to hide the tear that slipped down her cheek. There was still so much she had to tell him. And the next thing, she feared, he would never forgive her for. But, she needed this time with him now, just to be held tight in his arms. Before the night was over he may never want to speak to her again. And they'd be right back to where they left off.

CHAPTER 9

"He didn't sell this house. I know he didn't sell it. He's too damned sentimental to part with a damned beer mug we won at the fall festival ten years ago, he didn't sell this house." Galen said as he pulled another trinket from one of the boxes he'd pulled down from the attic.

JJ looked up from the box she was going through. "You sold it to him."

"I was doing a few insane things back then."

"Like winning a gold glove."

"You knew?"

"I knew, or I heard later." She said.

"Where did you go JJ? Other than the places you've documented so very well."

"All over. I saw you on television sometimes when I could find one." She dove back into the box of pictures she was going through, and held up a picture of him sticking his tongue out, which for a while was his favorite pose.

"Such a sincere thinker huh?" He tossed a seashell over his shoulder as he rummaged through old mementos.

Galen moved one box to the side and pulled up another. He opened it and found a worn glove and some photos. JJ toes wiggled as she stretched. He reached out and grabbed the toe ring.

"You still have this?"

Jill was silent for a moment. "It's my good luck charm, I've taken it off only twice." She frowned and threw her thumb over her back. "It won't come off again."

"I can't believe you kept it."

"You gave it to me. Did you want it back?"

"I gave you another one you could have kept, you didn't have to give it back."

"Yes, I did, it wasn't mine anymore." She didn't look up, she just kept sorting through things. "If he did sell this house, I wonder if the new owners will sell it to me?"

"Get in line, but I know Bobby, he could no more sell this house than keep his nose out of my business."

"He's a good friend Galen."

"I know." Galen reached into the bottom of the box in front of him and pulled out a framed photograph of himself and JJ when the world was still something to be explored and their lives were blissfully ahead of them. The couple only had eyes for each other, and they were sharing an intimate joke. He knew exactly what he'd just said to put the little bit of color in her cheeks just before Bobby snapped the shot. A snippet of Bobby's finger was in the corner of the picture. He turned the picture around to face JJ. "We were so damned young then. We had nothing but this old house and whatever we could bring in working part time. But I think we were pretty happy. Poor, but happy."

Jill looked at the framed picture wistfully. "Do you remember the first meal we I made, for you and Bobby?" The picture had been taken shortly after they finished eating it on the redwood table that still sat grayed and weathered in the yard.

"You made chicken and biscuits, and corn on the cob that was so close to the Colonel's recipe that we couldn't tell the difference." He winked. "Because there was no difference. You hid the bucket and bag in the trash."

"After I burned the macaroni and cheese I was going to serve you guys that night. You set me up, daring me to cook for you, and I took the bait. Thank God that didn't last long."

"Thank God is right, the smoke alarm went off every time you got near the stove."

"The way I figure it, you burn a few things, no one asks you to cook for them anymore, I think it was a flawless plan." Jill lifted her chin and smirked. "Besides, who wants to spend hours cooking when the two of you would eat the cardboard box the pizza came in if you were hungry enough?"

"You burned things on purpose? You ruined how many pots and pans?"

"It took a while, and it might have taken less time if I hadn't tried to redeem myself after that first attempt by spending a week's grocery money on the KFC." She snorted, "When you and Bobby told me I was elected the cook, I figured I'd un-elect myself. And it worked."

"I knew it! You faked being a bad cook." He looked at the picture again.

"You told me that there were other rooms in the house I had talent in." She blushed again. "And I almost felt guilty about burning the meals I did after that." A gleam played in her eyes. "But not that guilty."

"So it seems I was deluded into thinking you couldn't cook at all. Well 'Ms. I can't cook so don't ask me', I think you'll have to show me exactly how much talent I missed all those years. Is there anything else you need to get off of your chest?"

Jill's smile faded to a faraway forced grin. "No, not…" She lifted her head to see him searching through the bottom of the box. "I'll see what I can do, I'm really not that good in the kitchen though."

"For what it's worth, I think you're very good in every room of the house." He said and grinned.

Some of the memorabilia he'd pushed around the box stirred memories of long hot nights in the dead of winter, and holding on to one another as if there was no one else in the world. There was a piece of leather that broke off of his glove that he wrapped around her slim wrist, promising her a real bracelet for Christmas. There were a few dozen love notes from her that he'd caught hell from his old team about, but he never parted with a single one. There was her Friday bikini brief; black lace with the day of the week embroidered over the front in red. The two red bows that held the sides together were tied now, but he knew exactly how easy it had been to tug that ribbon open and slide into heaven. His body remembered that it hadn't been long since he'd been there, and now it was begging for a return trip.

Jill caught a glimpse of what was in the box he was going through. Her heart watched his fingers toy with the frilly black lace she knew was hers.

"I ugh…" he looked up and smiled.

She bit her lips together. "Please don't tell me you kept Monday through Thursday too?"

"No, just Friday. I liked Friday. I still like Friday." Bolder now, he held the lace up. "Although the purple Wednesdays were a big turn on too."

"You remember that?"

"Not until just now."

"If the broiler works, that steak in the freezer will go bad with the electricity off and all…" She couldn't breath right again. He was staring at her like she was on the menu, and as much as she wanted to let him order, there was no way they could have a repeat of this afternoon's encounter on the stairs yet. She headed for the kitchen.

"I'll be down in a minute to help." He said. *After I'm able to stand up and walk.*

He saw the desire burning in her eyes, it was as plain as day, but the sadness and doubt he saw just before that puzzled him. This afternoon was the result of chemistry that hadn't changed, or faded. He couldn't be in the same room with her without thinking about holding her, touching her, being inside of her. *Reclaiming her as his.* And where the hell did that thought come from? But that's what it had been, again. He claimed her all those years ago, and she was his, her body only knew him, and it was right, so right, he'd forgotten himself in her, and it was as if he'd died and gone to heaven. Again.

    Galen pulled another box close and opened it leaning it toward the dull light coming through the window. It was filled with books, old magazines, and papers.

    Bobby's things.

He pulled open an old issue of Playboy, and decided against paging through it for safety's sake and his sanity. He tossed it back into the box and pushed it aside when a few letters addressed to JJ slid forward. There were four in all, and none had been opened. They were from a medical clinic in Israel. He dug deeper and found another letter unopened from someplace in Lebanon, the address was hand written but smeared. The glue had hardened and peeled, so a corner of the envelope was opened, and just by him handling it, the center of the flap opened.

This was JJ's stuff, and it was none of his business. Why hadn't Bobby ever told him that these letters had come for her? They were postmarked over six years ago. He turned the envelope over and the contents spilled out with a handwritten letter. It was from a woman JJ had known in Lebanon.

He could barely make out words in the scrawled writing. It looked foreign, like the writer was battling with the words and the pen. He picked up a card that fell out with the letter, and his heart sank. The name Galen Robert McInnes LeBuntoski was printed in the same scrawled writing beneath a small footprint.

The footprint of a baby. JJ had a baby.

His mind filled with chaos as he sifted through the rest of the papers and did his best to decipher the words written on them. Temper rising, he tore through sheets of medical reports until he found a crude birth certificate with his son's name on it and some dates...nat. 12/31...mort. 12/31. The pain that shot through him when he realized what the paper was saying was sharper than a knife wound. Math hadn't been his forte, but the child described on that paper was his. He had a son.

JJ had his baby in a foreign country, and never bothered to tell him she was pregnant. The baby died, and apparently JJ had almost died as well from what he could make of the woman's writing. Bile rose in his throat as he tried to make sense of the notes.

Galen closed his eyes fighting anger and loss. He read on…thirty hours of unproductive labor brought on by trauma…massive hemorrhaging...concussion…His head was spinning with each word he read.

JJ had been alone, except for the nurse who wrote the note wishing her happiness, and telling her in not so perfect English that she hoped one day she and JJ could shed tears of joy together rather than the tears of sadness they'd spilled.

A hundred questions skidded through his brain. What the hell was she thinking putting herself and *their* baby, *his* baby in danger? And what the hell happened?

He should have been there. No, she should have been here, with him, in an American hospital seeing the best doctors money could buy. Then…then what? According to the nurse, there was nothing that could have been done.

There sure as hell could have been something done, he could have been there with her, had she bothered to tell him about the baby!

He scanned the scattered paperwork again. It happened on New Years Eve, where the hell had he been back then? His mind raced through past celebrations to the first one he'd had without JJ.

He was on the beach with Philippa Jutsen, the model who he thought for sure would cure him of JJ. He remembered hoping that wherever JJ was she'd been watching the Wild and Single Show the entertainment network had been taping after following him around for a few days. He made a point of practically making a porn flick out of the segment in hopes that it would show JJ he'd gone on without her, and didn't need her in his life. His eyes closed in embarrassment and frustration now. He hoped that she missed it.

Chances were pretty good that she did. She was too busy having his baby, a baby that almost killed her. His thoughts moved to the stairway, and her reaction later.

He couldn't breathe, couldn't think. For so many years he hadn't felt anything, now he was overload with it all. Anger, fear, loss, and unfathomable sadness coursed through him like a raging river out of control, his whole body shook.

"She didn't tell me, she didn't trust me enough to tell me. How the hell much did she think I didn't want her for her to hold this in?" Tears fell onto the yellowed paper he folded and placed back in the envelope. Then he studied the footprint again. His child, a son, never took a single breath. And the woman he loved had to have been in hell, alone.

He stared down at the footprint. "She must have held you, your mom would have held you." And she had let go alone. Or had she let go at all? He tucked the card into his shirt pocket unable to part with it yet.

Glass Elevators

Galen pushed the box aside, ignoring the chill that set in away from the fire. He took a long look at the framed picture of the two of them. The girl in the picture would have shared the news with him, she would have never left, but the jackass in the picture forced her hand.

"…If you're not here…don't bother to come back." His words spoken in desperation haunted him. Where the hell else could she go? She had no one but him and Bobby, and he'd told her not to come back. If the situation were reversed, he'd have done the same and stayed away. But it wasn't reversed. His star had been rising, and he hadn't taken off knowing…did she know she was pregnant when she left?

He dug through the box again looking for something, anything that would tell him for sure. He found it, a receipt for a pregnancy test, from the medical clinic in Israel. Two months after she left. She had no idea that she was carrying his baby when she walked out the door.

But he knew.

He knew in his heart that she was pregnant, even before she left.

No, not before she *left.*

Before he abandoned her.

CHAPTER 10

Snow banked against the house. The steps leading up to the porch disappeared. Cold winds blowing through the open porch door cooled his blood. It was dark now, yet he could still make out smoke billowing from the chimney across the street and a flicker of light from the window, probably from a candle or hurricane lamp. He craned his neck to look down the street, a thick white blanket of snow and ice covered the landscape, there was no telling where the sidewalk ended and the street began. Snow blew and swirled into the porch, there was a fine lacy layer covering the wicker chairs and the tarp he covered the stack of firewood with.

It didn't look like they'd be going anywhere anytime soon. Galen lifted some split logs into his arms and carried them into the front room, shutting the door behind him with his foot. The wind whistled in protest. He put a few logs next to the fireplace, and tossed two into the snapping fire. His thoughts scattered like the sparks. Absently, he lit another candle to add to the golden light from the fireplace. They would spend the night here, in the living room in front of the fire. The rest of the house was getting cold without the heat and boiler running.

The sound of JJ singing made his heart jump. She sounded relaxed and content, a vast contrast to the way his emotions were jumping around now. She had years to come to terms with all he'd just learned. He pulled the small card out of his pocket and read the name again. JJ wanted this baby, *his* baby; she kept him even after she thought she couldn't come home. He tucked the card back into his pocket and stared at the kitchen door.

The kitchen was warm and smelled wonderful. Candles lit the small space, and created an amber glow that fit the warmth and aromas. The smothered steak was just about ready, the potatoes mashed by hand with real butter, fresh pepper and a hint of garlic looked perfect. Honeyed carrots added sweetness to the air. JJ found a bottle of wine, and tossing all caution to the wind, which was still howling, she popped the cork. Filling a blue glass bowl with fresh snow, she nestled the bottle in it to chill. What the heck was taking Galen so long? Just about an hour ago he said he'd be down to help, not that she was counting on it, but it was puzzling that he hadn't even poked his nose in once, just to make sure she wasn't setting the place on fire.

JJ stepped back and looked at the cozy scene; it struck her like a slap in the face. What if she'd never left? Would this be just another meal they'd be sharing together? Tears came to her eyes as the third chair drew her attention, maybe that chair would have been filled now with a little boy awaiting his dinner. Oh God! JJ blinked furiously to chase the thoughts away.

She should tell him. But how could she tell him without risking what they'd begun to mend? He would blame her for losing their son, and he would be right.

Maybe he'd think it was for the best. That thought hurt more than the first. She closed her eyes and made a decision. After they had dinner, they'd talk, and she'd tell him, then live with the consequences. Maybe tomorrow the storm would let up, and she could leave and never have to see him again, he certainly wouldn't want to see her after her confession.

Searching for another potholder, she found an old transistor radio. When she turned the knob, it came to life. The low battery light was on, but for now it was a distraction she needed. She sang along with the static and poured some chilled wine into her glass.

Galen's gaze fell over the small round table lit with two tall candles. Light sparkled off of the blue bowl holding a bottle of wine and the balloon glasses she'd set next to mismatched plates. One glass, he noticed, was only partially full.

"I thought you might be hungry, I found some canned carrots, mushrooms and potatoes." She still hadn't looked at him, but her voice went up a notch. "I didn't burn anything, the smoke detectors operate on batteries, so you'd know. I thought that maybe you were waiting until one of them went off to come down."

The aromas that danced around him called to his lost appetite. She cooked for him, when being in this kitchen couldn't possibly be easy for her. Hell being in this house had to hurt. But, she'd never taken the easy way out of anything, including her work. JJ was right though, they weren't the same people they had been. Anger melted, sorrow struck again. How could he ask her the questions he needed answers to now?

She stopped scurrying around the kitchen and turned to face him. Concern etched her face as she approached him, her hand reached for his cheek in a familiar soothing gesture. "Galen are you ok?"

It was more than he could bear. He took her hand before she touched him, and pulled her in, holding her like he'd never be able to let go. His body shook when she embraced him back.

"You're scaring me…what happened? What's the matter?" She asked.

"JJ, I'm…I'm so sorry Sweetheart, you should have come home when you found out. You could have come home, this was your home as much as mine, but I told you not to come back, I didn't mean it, why didn't you call, or write? I would have come to get you, you shouldn't have been alone then JJ." She pushed away from him, fear made her tremble.

"Galen what are you talking about?" Her breaths were ragged, and panic was in close pursuit. She closed her eyes and willed calm, she was good at evading her worst enemy no matter how close he came. Panic wouldn't take over, couldn't take over, she wouldn't allow it.

The mask she drew over her face was surreal, the transformation frightening. Galen reached for her and touched her cheek, her skin was cool, her eyes muddy. This was PJ Storm, the photojournalist with ice in her veins. This is how she did it, the same way she dealt with her stepmother, and everything unpleasant in her life, she shut down.

His heart broke again, she wasn't alone anymore though, he wouldn't let her shut him out again.

He held out the card with a tiny footprint on it. "JJ, I want to know about my son. Our son."

Her mask melted slowly, but not without a battle. Her face paled so that it was noticeable in the amber light. She staggered back and reached for a chair, he caught her arm, guiding her into the seat. Whatever control she mastered wavered and emotion overcame her massive effort. She buried her face in her hands and sobbed so hard that the table shook with her. He stroked her hair, and kissed the top of her head, kneeling down to next to her.

"Oh God." She sobbed. "Oh Galen, I'm so sorry. I wanted to tell you, I was going to tell you, I wanted to wait until after we ate something. I was…it hurts still."

He held her, and felt the echoes of pain that vibrated through her into him.

"JJ it's ok, it's going to be ok." He hushed her and stroked her hair.

"It's not ok Galen, no matter how many times I try to tell myself it is, it's not. It's all my fault."

"No JJ, not according to the nurse who wrote to you. I found a letter with this in an old box Bobby packed." She lifted her tear-streaked face, sobs racked her body. "You could have died JJ, and that would have been *my* fault."

Shaking, she stared at him and spoke through hiccupping sobs. "Did you set the bomb off in the restaurant? Did you have so much damned pride that you wouldn't admit you needed help?"

Galen straightened as if he'd been slapped. "I don't understand what you're talking about."

Glass Elevators

It took her a few more minutes to gather enough breath to speak again. "I went to work the day before the baby was due. Tamar begged me not to, she said it was close to my time, and it was too dangerous. But I was broke and already in her debt. I lost my grant after I started showing, but I couldn't come back here, I had nothing to come back to. You didn't want me, and if you didn't want me, how could you want our baby? And I wanted him." She wrapped both arms around her belly and rocked away from him. Galen moved and gathered her in his arms, she was tearing his heart to shreds.

"You were doing so well, and I would have been the lost girl on your doorstep again, with a baby no less? I couldn't do that." She sniffed and wiped at the tears that flowed. "It was just a regular day, I was cooking in the back room…cooking…me that's a laugh right? I finished cleaning out a tray, and the first cramp hit me. A delivery came and a man I'd never seen before set a package down by the doorway to the dining area and left." She gulped a sob. "Then another contraction came and my water broke. A burst of heat knocked me over, and then I was in the hospital, and Tamar was standing over me, holding my hand and praising God that I was still alive."

"I was still…" she looked away, "I remember thinking how smart the baby was, he waited until we were in the hospital to make his appearance." She pressed her lips together to stifle a sob. "I was wrong, he was already gone. The blast…" She stopped and grabbed a napkin to wipe her face.

"Oh, JJ what did I do to you?" His tears flowed into her hair as he held her close.

"For a long time I blamed you. After I saw that video of you on the beach, I hated you. But it was me, the one thing I wanted to be good at, more than any thing else, and I failed completely from the start." She looked into his red eyes. "I didn't know how to tell you, I didn't know if…I didn't find out I was pregnant until after I left you Galen, and by then…"

"By then you were convinced I didn't want anything to do with you." He finished for her, barely choking the words out.

"You were moving on, and doing all of the things you dreamed of, your name was in the headlines, you were a success. You didn't need an anchor slowing you down."

Her last statement hurt more than anything else she'd said. How many times did he give her the George Bailey line… 'shaking the dust from this old town…'

"Not all of the things I dreamed of. Without you, the dreams were empty." He said, his words barely a whisper.

She looked away unable to accept his kindness. "I lost the one thing I'd have gladly given everything to have." She stopped sobbing, and a veil was falling over her face again. "They never found the group that claimed responsibility for the bomb. There were some leads, but I couldn't find them."

Galen heard her words through his haze, but it took a minute for them to sink in. Was she still looking for the terrorists responsible for the bomb that killed their baby?

"I don't care who was responsible for the bomb. I was responsible for you, and I failed you. You didn't fail JJ. You did what you thought was right." He held her face in his hands. "I should have known, I knew it, felt it. I knew you were pregnant, I even hoped you were, so you wouldn't go." He kissed her cheek. "I should have known what that grant meant to you and supported you, because you would have come back. You would have come home, you would have known it was ok, and you never would have doubted how much I love you."

His last words stunned her. Looking into his eyes made her believe he meant them, he had loved her.

"I still love you JJ." He answered her unasked question. "I'm not sure I ever stopped. Even if you can't forgive me, don't shut me out. Don't hide from me the way you want to now."

Her head snapped back, she had been sliding into her control mode again, it was the only way to block out the pain, the grief, and now the longing he stirred in her. He was holding her again, sharing grief she'd carried for too long. "I can't help it Galen, it still hurts. There's not a day that goes by that I don't think about him."

"I know it hurts, I want to help I just don't know what to do. My heart is in pieces JJ, I can't begin to imagine how you coped. I'm sorry I wasn't there for you, I know that doesn't make it better. I don't know how to make it better, I wish I did."

A shrill whine pierced the quiet and had them both spinning. Apparently the batteries in the smoke detector were working just fine.

"Oh no!" She grabbed the pot of honey glazed carrots off of the stove and tossed it into the sink. Steam billowed up from the pot as water hit the burned vegetables. JJ bit her lower lip, then spun to face Galen. "I burned the carrots." She cried again, knowing that it was ridiculous to be so upset over carrots.

"It's ok, we burned the carrots sweetheart, but the steak looks perfect, and I think the mashed potatoes look, umm," He lifted the masher and the pot lifted up with it. "They'll be fine."

She smiled through her tears, and even let out a small chuckle. She was an emotional train wreck.

"Oh Galen, I wanted this day to come so many times, I thought about how I'd tell you, and what, and none of what I thought is right. I hurt you, and you're still telling me my stupid mashed potatoes are fine? You're supposed to be mad, or glad or yell, I don't know."

He braced his arms on the counter trapping her close to the sink, his eyes leveled with hers. "I am. I'm all of that. I'm mad I couldn't be there for you, mad that I was so young and stupid to let you go without you knowing how much you meant to me. Mad that I didn't find you, mad I didn't let myself look enough, and madder still that we lost so much time. But I'm glad you told me, and glad you're here now with me, and very glad you didn't shoot me on sight. I want to yell, and scream and curse the powers that be for keeping us apart and letting us hurt each other the way we have, but maybe we need this storm, we need to be here now so we can fix this. Bobby was right, and I didn't see it until now."

He was just inches from her, his breath warmed her cheeks. Somewhere inside of him a fire was burning itself out, like the flames within her that had smoldered for too long.

"You're not alone anymore JJ." He whispered so low she wasn't sure that she heard him.

"Neither are you Galen." She whispered back.

The room was silent as they absorbed all that was said and left unsaid.

"I'm sorry JJ, so sorry I can't even explain it."

"I'm sorry too." She hugged him, then reached up and wrapped her arms around his neck and held on, whispering in his ear what she'd never told another living soul. "He was beautiful. Ten fingers and toes, and dark hair like you." She sniffed again. "They let me hold him and name him, they didn't want to, but I…I just hope he knew I loved him."

"Oh Sweetheart, he knew." He closed his eyes, and pictured her holding the tiny infant. "He knew."

"I didn't want to give him up even when I knew he was gone."

"It's ok now. You're ok JJ."

"I named him Galen, but I thought that if you ever had a son with someone else…you might name him Galen Michael, so I used Robert, I couldn't face hearing about a little boy with the same name as our baby." She sniffed, somehow sharing her deepest secret with him felt right, as if he was getting to know the child he never touched.

"I think it's a good name, thank you." He blew out a long shaky breath.

Together they held on and weathered the storm of emotions spinning through them until calm settled in.

The bottle of wine clanked against the side of the glass bowl now filled with water.

"Are you ok?" He asked her pulling back enough to see her face.

She nodded, then hiccupped hard. "I'm a messy crier." She wiped her drying tears away and struggled with a change of subject. "The steak is probably cold now."

"I'll warm it up, have some of the wine you poured." He kissed her forehead.

"I will, I just want to…I need a minute. I'll be right back." She said.

She hesitated then pushed through the kitchen door, a few minutes later he heard water running through the old pipes. Galen turned the oven back on and placed the steak in a dish with the gravy and mushrooms. He reheated the potatoes with some milk and butter added, and pounded them into a fluffy cloud again. The carrots were a complete loss, he dumped the contents into the garbage, and set the pot in water to soak. Leaning heavily on the counter, he closed his eyes for a moment, struggling against frustration and the 'could have beens' that raced through his head. He was drained as if he'd gone ten rounds with a heavy weight champ.

  JJ looked up into the bathroom mirror; a candle on the counter flickered, casting shadows over her face. She certainly didn't look like a cool collected businesswoman. Hell, she didn't even resemble the drab forgettable PJ Storm. She looked like a mess. Her eyes were puffy and red as her nose. She cupped her hands under the icy water and held it to her face until she needed air.

When she looked in the mirror again, she felt better, lighter, like she could finally take a deep breath, and the air was cleaner. She toweled off, brushed her hair and changed out of the shirt she'd dripped tears on.

Galen was squatting by the fireplace adding wood to the fire when she returned. Firelight danced over his face highlighting his eyes, and shadowing the day old stubble on his chin.

"It's cold upstairs." Her voice startled him, he turned to face her. She stole his breath. A soft white sweater hugged her curves. Black jeans and thick wooly gray socks, probably weren't supposed to look as sexy but they did on JJ, she looked gorgeous.

"The food smells good." She started toward the kitchen and stopped. "Thank you, for listening, and for being here."

"I'm not going anywhere JJ." Pulling her into his arms he kissed the top of head and again drank in the scent of her. How did he live without this for so long?

Dinner didn't interfere with their long conversation. As coffee heated in an old blue spattered enamel pot on the stove, the aroma filled the room while Galen washed, rinsed and handed each clean dish and pot to JJ to dry. When the last glass was put away and coffee was poured they retreated to the warmth of the fireplace. Galen brought the small radio with them after finding replacement batteries in a drawer stuffed with odds and ends.

Sparks jumped and sizzled when JJ added another heavy log to the fire. Galen positioned the couch closer to the hearth, and lit another candle.

"We should spend the night here. It's cold up stairs. I know heat rises and all, but I don't think it'll rise enough to keep the whole floor warm." He watched for a reaction from her, they'd spoken freely through dinner and clean up, and it had become easy again. He didn't want tension between them. "You can sleep on the couch JJ."

She turned to face him a smile tugged at her lips. "I'll get the blankets and pillows, if you get some more wood off of the porch."

"Deal." He tried not to look surprised, but he didn't expect her to agree so readily.

She'd talked to Galen about her work, places she's been, things she's seen, good and bad, and he listened. He told her about the playoffs and people he met, charity work he's involved with, and after finishing a glass of wine and refusing more, he told her about his drinking. It wasn't an easy thing for him to admit, Galen liked control, and his drinking had started to control him. He told her he was going to do something about it. She figured he had just taken the first step.

She felt very different from the woman who pulled up in front of the house just yesterday. Lighter, like layers of lead chains had been cut away.

JJ quickly changed into a pair of warm sweats and a flannel sleep shirt, then pulled the wool socks back over her toes, the bare floor was cold. She lifted her bedding and tossed it all down the steps.

When she opened the door to Galen's room she froze, it was like walking into the past again. It still held his scent, all masculine and spicy with a hint of leather and musk. She inhaled deeply. JJ glanced at the bed, blankets were folded at the bottom, they were the one thing that was different than she remembered. A familiar frame on the dresser caught her eye, but it was empty. Once it held a picture of her, now the glass was broken. The lamp was the same, the chip in it from a pillow fight they'd had still prominent. In the corner was a wooden chair she spent a few nights in watching Galen sleep after a concussion diagnosis. Waking him every two hours like the doctor told her to, she spent the time in between praying for him to be ok, because he was just starting to live his dream.

    JJ sat on the edge of his bed and reached for the nightstand, then drew back as if it might bite her. She had no right to look. Her hand brushed over the unfamiliar blankets, reminding her that he had lived here after she'd gone. Her things remained unchanged because they weren't used, his were. The thought of another woman in his bed, sharing his body drew her back to the present. She lifted the blankets and brought them to her face, his scent was still there too.

Galen kicked off his work boots inside the door, and stacked the wood by the fireplace. When he heard something tumble down the steps, he flew to the landing, thinking she was tangled in the mess. He was relived to find only blankets and pillows. Bedding that reached out to him as if she just walked into the room. He held the blankets to his nose, her essence penetrated his soul. A smile crossed his lips when he detected his own cologne mixed in. He'd spent hours sitting watching her sleep last night, dying to crawl into the bed with her, even if it was just to protect her from the ghosts that haunted her dreams.

He tossed the blankets on the couch and waited for more bedding to rain down, when it didn't, he went up. The door to his room was ajar, he watched from the hallway as she explored, and remembered. She reached for the drawer to his nightstand, and a prickle of dread nagged him. If Bobby hadn't moved anything, her ring was still sitting in the corner, next to a box of condoms.

He had to move the ring box purposely to get to the condoms, a reminder to keep it light, commitments were unacceptable. Relief swept its wings over his heart as she pulled away, there were probably a few souvenirs from his post JJ romps in that drawer too.

She frowned as she stroked the blankets. The one she made for him was in the closet, he couldn't bear having it wrapped around him while he was wrapped around someone else.

"I kept it JJ." Pulling her handmade quilt from the top shelf of his old closet, Galen opened the door wide. The small door that lead to her closet was in there too, hidden behind some old jerseys.

"I got distracted." She smiled and shrugged. "It is really getting cool up here."

She grabbed the pillow and walked out the door, leaving him with a crazy quilt made by the love of his life. It said so, stitched on the lining, right next to the words, *to keep you warm while chasing your dreams*. He smiled, he was still chasing one of his dreams, because she just walked down the stairs.

A loud crash shook the ground startling JJ and had Galen jumping to the landing from mid stairway.

"What do you think that was?" JJ went to the front window. From what little she could see, nothing looked out of place. "It sounded like it came from the side of the house."

One look out that window had her cringing. Her car was buried under the big pine that had grown forever on the patch of yard alongside the driveway. It gave in to the heavy snow that covered its branches weighing the tree down. Galen's truck looked to be buried too. He stood behind her wincing.

"I guess I'm going to have to buy Henry a new truck." When she looked at him over her shoulder he elaborated. "I had to borrow my neighbor's truck to get here, my car wouldn't start."

Her heart flip-flopped in her chest. He borrowed a ride because he thought she needed him.

"I think my car took the brunt of it, maybe the truck is just scratched."

He stared at her then laughed. "How will I be able to tell? Did you see the thing?"

She laughed with him, and found herself in his arms again.

CHAPTER 11

A thick blanket of snow covered the northeast. Snow was still falling, though the wind died down considerably. Phone lines and cell towers were damaged, and there were major power outages up and down the coastline.

Bobby stared out at a city that was quiet and strangely tranquil, and wondered if things were as quiet and tranquil one state over. He doubted it. In fact he hoped to hell the storm there was still raging. Maybe then his friends could find peace. He might not have their friendship after the stunt he pulled, but it would all be worth it if they both survived.

He tossed an old baseball in the air and caught it, then spun it to look at Galen's name scribbled across the front. It was his first major league homerun ball, and he'd given it to Bobby and called him the closest thing he ever had to a brother.

"Well Bro, I hope you and JJ find something up there worth living for." He put the ball back on his mantle, and climbed into bed. Maybe tonight he'd get some sleep.

"There's nothing we can do about the tree until the snow stops." Galen said. He looked down at JJ and reminded himself that they'd only just found each other again a few hours ago, yet this moment felt so right, so natural.

"I don't think it's going to stop anytime soon." JJ said. It was a small miracle that she was back in Galen's arms again.

"You know I really don't mind. In fact, I can't think of a place I'd rather be, or a person I'd rather be spending time with." He said.

"You mean that?" She pulled back to look into his face. "After everything I've told you?"

"I mean that." He looked away for a moment, "I wish we could have done things differently."

"I do too." She closed her eyes and wished away years of regret. "But, maybe we can still…"

"There's no maybe JJ. I'm not losing you again." He dialed down his determined tone and took a breath. "Look, there are things we both did that we're going to have to get over, but I think we can."

JJ wanted to believe that, wanted nothing more than to give *them* another chance, there was so much still to think about, and talk about, and get through.

"We aren't the same people we were Gale."

He couldn't help the smile, or the way his heart thudded against his ribs while he was just holding her there, hearing her say his name. "Thank God for that."

CHAPTER 12

"No. That contract was settled last week, there's no provision for…" Bobby spun in his chair and nearly choked. "…I'll call you back." He ended the call, and swallowed hard. Neither person standing in his office looked happy, and if either of them were armed, he was in deep shit.

"Just what the hell did you think you were doing?"

"Did you really think that by throwing us together in a stinking blizzard was going to change anything?"

"I uh…" Bobby sputtered.

"Don't think that we didn't figure it out." JJ shook her finger at him.

"You owe me pal." Galen glared then bared his teeth as he spoke. "And on this, I definitely intend to collect."

"No heat, no electricity, cut off from everything for four days. Are you aware of what that can do to two people?" JJ stopped pacing and leaned over Bobby's desk looming inches from his face.

"What the hell were you thinking?" Galen growled.

"Did you think that we'd actually be able to put everything behind us? Move on? Forgive and forget?" JJ asked.

"Well I…" Bobby started to answer, not sure what he'd actually say.

"I can't believe you'd do something like that Bobby, I trusted you." JJ said.

"You actually thought that you were helping, didn't you?" Galen said. "Thought if we just spent some time together, that everything would work out, we'd talk things out, listen to each other…"

"…And realize what idiots we've been." JJ finished his sentence.

"I…" Bobby thought he heard an admission somewhere in all the yelling, he replayed the last accusation in his head, and noticed a small grin tugging at his friends' lips. "Idiots you've been?"

"I thought we agreed on pig headed and stubborn." Galen pulled JJ over to his side, and wrapped his arms around her small frame.

"I ad-libbed." JJ said then kissed Galen on the cheek.

Bobby couldn't believe his eyes, he hoped it wasn't some kind of joke. "I hate you both right now, but if I'm really seeing what I think I am, I couldn't be a happier man."

"Did you see his face when we first walked in?" Galen snickered, holding Jill close.

"Worth rehearsing for, I should have brought my camera."

"Sure, fine. Thanks." Bobby was at a loss. His plan worked, now the big question was, for how long?

JJ and Galen took the seats opposite Bobby's desk, holding hands like they never wanted to let go again.

"So you kissed and made up?" Bobby asked tentatively.

The couple smiled as if they had a secret, which was infinitely better than snarling and snapping at him, or each other, or worse; ignoring each other.

"I'd say we reached an agreement." Galen squeezed JJ's hand as he spoke, a hand that donned an opal ring surrounded by tiny diamonds.

"When you both dropped off the face of the earth for three weeks, I figured I really screwed up. Jeanine didn't know where you went, or what happened, except that one of you wanted to buy the house."

"We, took a little trip after being snowbound for a few days." JJ said. "He showed me his, and I showed him mine." She laughed. "We want to buy back what's ours Bobby, so that it's all of ours. The three of us, so that it'll always be a home for us."

"You do know I had no intention of really selling it?" Bobby tossed out.

"We kinda figured that out, but, if you let both of us own a piece of it too, we'll always have it." Galen said while looking at JJ as if she was the only one in the room with him.

"Works for me." Bobby sat back in his chair and studied the couple. "I'm guessing you've talked."

"We…yea." Galen said.

"So he knows about your alter ego?" Bobby directed at JJ.

"Yes, but he's not so comfortable with PJ yet." JJ squeezed Galen's hand as she spoke. "We've kinda-sorta worked a few things out." JJ looked over at Galen and there was no mistaking the look in her eyes.

Stasha definitely owed him dinner and he couldn't wait to collect.

"We may need your help." Galen mentioned casually, "We tied the knot last weekend in Vegas. We need to transfer some things and figure out some paperwork, and you know, the usual just married stuff."

Bobby couldn't be more shocked if someone told him he'd won the lottery. He figured the two of them would get together, but not this together, this soon.

"Hellooo?" JJ said waving her hand in front of Bobby's stunned face.

Bobby snapped back to the new reality that he had a hand in creating. "I uh…"

"Great, the man of a thousand words is rendered speechless." Galen said.

"Does anyone else know?" Bobby sputtered.

"Only the priest at St. Maria's, and Stasha." Galen answered. "We would have notified you, but you weren't taking any calls at that particular time. Care to explain that Mr. Harris?" Galen asked, knowing the only reason Bobby turned his phone off.

"Not particularly. You want the public to get a hold of this yet?" Bobby asked, and both of them shook their heads, then stared at one another.

"Please don't tell me he represents you." They both asked simultaneously.

"Only the best for my friends" Bobby said.

Glass Elevators

CHAPTER 13

Jill sat on the steps and gazed across the bay and nearly burst with joy. Bundled up against the late March breeze, cup of coffee in hand, she scanned the newspaper. Deciding she didn't want to read about anything that might alter her bright mood, she turned to the comics. The decaf wasn't quite giving her the kick she was used to, but it would have to do, she wasn't taking any chances. She turned to the sports pages, and lo and behold her handsome husband was staring back at her with a broad grin under the headline; New York's Big Mac Attack!

He'd hit four homeruns in his last three preseason games, and was leading his new team in RBIs. Not a bad start for spring. Her heart did a little jig in her chest. He looked happy, really happy. He sounded happy last night when he called, except for the relentless campaigning he did for her to join him in Florida for the remainder of spring training. It's not like she wasn't considering it, it was just that maybe some space right now wasn't such a bad thing, she needed to do some heavy thinking. The kind she had a hard time doing with Galen around distracting her.

When he read her new series that was slated for publication about the same time as opening day, he was going to go ballistic. This time she couldn't blame him.

Glass Elevators

She'd been scared too. Jill hoped that her news might temper his reaction; she just had to keep her secret one more week. Even if he did over react, she'd have to agree with him, there was no way she would let anything happen to their baby this time. He knew she went to Haiti on a humanitarian mission, he didn't know and neither did she what she seemed destined to stumble into. The way she seemed to be able to find trouble even when she wasn't looking for it lately was starting to niggle at her conscience.

It's not that she regretted her last adventure; she only hoped the article would stir a public outcry for change, and justice. A picture paints a thousand words, and some of those unspoken words still chilled her now even as she tried to banish them from her mind's eye with the beautiful scenery before her.

Glass Elevators

    She hadn't deliberately set out to put herself in harms way or open up a can of worms, which is an insult to worms everywhere. This time it just happened while she was deliberately trying to help the earthquake relief team her corporation sent in to aide the thousands of poor victims that were devastated by Mother Nature's wrath and were paying for it so long after the initial damage. Still he'd be upset when he saw the images she couldn't ignore exposing.

    As if he had some kind of radar on her thoughts, her cell phone went off indicating it was Galen. She tossed the paper down, and had to remind herself to be calm.

    A cool breeze flipped the paper open, fluttering past the entertainment section and the local news, stopping at World Events. There was a short article about two bodies found in a dump site. They appeared to have been dumped there after being shot in the back of the head. The bodies were tentatively identified as local merchants who were outspoken about the corruption plaguing their city and the relief efforts. Local authorities were still investigating the unfortunate incident.

The woman was impossible, she had insisted on traveling down to Haiti to help the earthquake victims who were still in dire need all this time after the quake hit. She promised to lie low, and play the role of Jillian Leigh, humanitarian and upper management of *I Did It Myself,* going down there to help with the relief effort, but every time her face appeared in a public venue she was opening herself up to being recognized as PJ Storm as far as he was concerned. She assured him that all of the major networks and news crews had moved on from their coverage of Haiti's plight even though so much assistance was still needed. And, she'd said as casually as if she was ordering a cup of coffee, no one had put two and two together in the six years PJ Storm existed.

He'd been monitoring the news, and only stopped when she called to tell him her plane had landed safely in New York. JJ had sounded exhausted so he cut his call short last night, but still hoped he could convince her to join him in Florida.

He mumbled JJ and put his cell to his ear and waited for her to pick up.

"Hi honey!" She said a bight too brightly, then toned down a notch. "Just saw your picture in the paper, 'His Majesty of Metropolis' is what the caption says."

He laughed into the phone. "I heard through Bobby that one of my thrones has been overflowing."

"Yea, we seem to have a bit of an issue with the castle's cesspool." JJ said, "I called a company Bobby recommended, it should be cleared up before you get home."

"I really wish you could just get away and come down here." He said keeping one eye on a rookie taking batting practice. "I guess it's a good thing you got home when you did though instead of stopping here first." He figured he's try to hit her with some guilt.

"It's only a few more days, and you'll be back in New York." JJ said, and noticed she had another call coming in, one she couldn't ignore. "I gotta run, I'll talk to you later." She disconnected and answered the call from a local rescue shelter she'd heard about.

After the last preseason game came to an end, Mac stared back at the reporter and counted to ten to rein in his temper. He demanded a smile, and his face responded, but he didn't feel the slightest bit happy. How the hell did this local yokel from a paper he'd never heard of find out about his marriage, or was the guy fishing?

"Word has it that you got married in the off season? You gonna introduce us to your bride?" The guy called out, then shot another question at him when deafening silence ensued. "You sold your house in LA and records show you *and* your *new wife* bought a house out on Long Island, so I'll assume you plan on staying in New York for a few years?"

"It's no secret Mr.?" Mac paused and waited for the tall lanky reporter to fill in the info again, he hadn't really paid attention to it the first time he announced it.

"Ken Burgess, North Coast Baseball Tribune." He said. Mac decided there was a hint of an accent there he couldn't place.

"Ken, I'm pretty sure the details of my contract are old news by now, most of you know more about it than I do." A wave of laughter rippled through the room. "I'm in New York for the long haul it would seem." Mac forced another grin, and added, "The commute from LA would be a killer."

Mac ended his stint at the mic as more questions rang out about is marital status. He shot a droll stare at the group that left them believing he still had a major aversion to monogamy.

Catcher Drew Madigan stepped up to the mic and addressed Mac as he was leaving, asking why he wasn't invited to the wedding or better yet when he'd missed the bachelor party. The room erupted in laughter as the guy cemented the opinion that Mac was still playing the field with a shake of his head and another joke. "I think one commitment per decade is all Mac can handle. And that was a tough sell, I had to agree to share my on camera time to get him to sign on the dotted line to come to New York."

Mac owed Drew big time. He just had to hold off the press for a bit longer, then he and Jillian Leigh would discretely acknowledge their marital status. He promised her that she'd have time to put enough barriers in place to keep some semblance of privacy in their lives. Her safety depended on it.

He finished packing his gear and cleaned up then dialed JJ to make sure she wouldn't be heading into the city for a meeting as he was heading out to their house after he landed on Long Island.

"Hey," JJ answered, "I was just thinking about you."

"Uh-oh." He said. "Is that good thinking about me, like I wonder how my awesome husband is doing? Or bad thinking, like the cesspool overflowed again and I'm up here having to deal with this on my own, and I'm going to punch him in the nose when I see him."

JJ laughed. "I think it's somewhere in between." She said. "But I do miss you. And you'll be happy to know that the cesspool problem has been dealt with."

"So, I'm not in the dog house?" He asked.

"No, but speaking of dog house…" JJ began.

"Ughhh, JJ..." Galen drew out his protest groan. "You know I'd love to get a dog, but we both are constantly traveling and it's not fair to the dog."

JJ was ready, he'd given her the opening she was hoping for. "Well, I've been thinking, what if one of us has decided to stay closer to home from now on."

Galen pulled the phone away from his ear and looked at it as if he misunderstood the words emanating from the speaker, then a smile too big for his face threatened to burst his cheeks.

"Jillian Jayne McInnes, you tell me right now if you are yanking my chain, or this is just some plot to get a puppy." He could barely contain his relief and happiness.

"Really? You really think I'd say something like that just to get a puppy?" She asked in mock surprise.

He thought about it for a minute, then decided she was being serious. He had to stop himself from doing cartwheels. "You mean it?"

JJ was laughing when she answered. "I mean it. Taking pictures of bunnies and puppies and drooling babies might be worth exploring."

Galen was rendered speechless. Before he found his voice, she was telling him that she had to go, but she'd see him when he got home because she was picking him up at Islip/MacArthur Airport, and had to get going.

JJ couldn't wait, she knew that she was acting like a little kid anxious to see her superhero, but she couldn't seem to hide her excitement. She had to concentrate while she was driving, which wasn't made easy with her new little friend riding shotgun. The mix breed pup sitting like a prince in the passenger seat with his tongue lolling out looked just as excited as she was. The little guy's tail hadn't stopped wagging since she'd picked him up two days earlier. Her smile only dimmed a tiny bit when she ran into a traffic jam on the Long Island Expressway which threatened to make her late. An hour and a half later, she and the pup had only traveled a few miles before traffic was flowing freely again. She pulled off to the side of Veteran's Highway when Galen called to tell her he landed and was heading to pick up his luggage. She assured him she'd be there in a few minutes.

JJ parked in short term parking, grabbed her little pal and almost made it to the doors when Mac met her on the sidewalk. One look at the pup had him laughing. He wrapped JJ in a bear hug then bent to pick up the puppy that looked like a real-life version of a young Pluto. "I knew it!" He bellowed as the puppy licked his face. This meant JJ was giving up living dangerously. He immediately fell in love with the brown eyed mush. "He's gonna be a big guy. Aren't you?" Galen asked the pup and looked at the size of his paws.

"I couldn't resist him." JJ said. "I figured since I'm going to be home most of the time, I might want some company." She shrugged and grabbed his small bag that had hit the sidewalk when he saw her. "And, anywhere I'm going I can probably take him with me."

Galen didn't want to interrupt, JJ seemed to be on a roll, he grabbed his rolling bag and followed her toward the parking lot hardly believing his ears, JJ had been doing some thinking it seemed, and he was thrilled with the results. The puppy followed along on the leash, holding a piece in his mouth like he was walking himself. Galen couldn't be happier if he tried. JJ was still talking as they got close to the car and she beeped it open. Galen put both bags in the trunk after handing JJ the leash. JJ picked up the puppy and held her breath for a moment, this was it, the moment she wanted to share with him for a lifetime.

"Does he have a name?" Galen asked as he opened the back door for her to put the puppy in. His eyes scanned the seat and land landed on the infant seat buckled in the back with a sign over it. *'To be filled in 6 months by a player to be named later'*

"We need to come up with more than one name Gale." JJ said and put the pup down. Galen's head turned so fast she thought he might have given himself whiplash. He lifted her off her feet and spun her around, then seemed to realize what he was doing and placed her down on her feet again as gently as he could. "You're ok? And all is good? And why didn't you tell me on the phone?"

JJ just looked up at him. "I figured this was better than a phone call."

"I love you!" He said and kissed any doubt she may have had away. "Much better."

The puppy barked with all of the excitement, and wound himself around the couple, then unwound himself and jumped up not wanting to miss anything.

They laughed as they watched the squirming bundle. "What was the name of that winter storm?"

"Yogi?" JJ answered wrinkling her nose. The puppy sat and looked up at them.

"Yogi is perfect for him." Galen said. "Perfect storm, perfect pup."

Glass Elevators

Made in the USA
Columbia, SC
13 April 2022